"Why did you decide to become a soldier?" Lexi asked.

"It was the right fit for me," Pierce said, gathering up his burger in both hands. "I wanted to serve and protect my country. After boot camp, I had a surprising aptitude for surveillance work. Maybe because I grew up in the mountains. Don't get me wrong, what I do is tough, but I love it. I believe in it."

Lexi's heart sighed. She couldn't help it. She thought of all the ways he met her impossible-to-meet criteria. He was a man of faith, he was committed and hardworking and devoted. He excelled at his job. He was close to his family. He was fun and easygoing and a can-do sort of man. He radiated integrity like the sun did light. In theory, he was exactly the right kind of guy.

Wouldn't you know it? The one man she actually liked wasn't looking for a commitment.

JILLIAN HART

grew up on her family's homestead, where she raised cattle, rode horses and scribbled stories in her spare time. After earning her English degree from Whitman College, she worked in travel and advertising before selling her first novel. When Jillian isn't working on her next story, she can be found puttering in her rose garden, curled up with a good book and spending quiet evenings at home with her family.

A Soldier for Keeps
Jillian Hart

Steeple Hill®

Published by Steeple Hill Books™

STEEPLE HILL BOOKS

**Steeple
Hill**®

Recycling programs
for this product may
not exist in your area.

ISBN-13: 978-0-373-87519-1
ISBN-10: 0-373-87519-3

A SOLDIER FOR KEEPS

Printed in U.S.A.

Direct my footsteps according to your word.
—*Psalms* 119:133

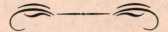

Chapter One

❧

"**M**ake way! Comin' through!" A man's shout rang behind her on the mountainside.

At the top of the run, Lexie Evans had just enough time to glance over her shoulder. A tall, muscled guy in black launched off the lift, dug in with his poles and flew toward her in a blur.

"Banzai!" His shout pierced the serene mountain quiet like gunfire. He was little more than a streak of black winging past. She caught the impression of a handsome profile, a shock of dark hair and an athletic physique as he shot down the run.

A daredevil type. She frowned, adjusting her goggles. She'd seen his kind before, sadly enough, and that made her raw heart ache. Romance had been hard on it. She thought she was over the strong burst of pain from her breakup with Kevin.

Okay, so she'd thought wrong. She dug in with her poles, ready to tackle the advanced grade run.

"Banzai!"

Here comes another one, she thought, looking over

her shoulder in time to see a second guy fly by in a blur of red. His cry was the same war note as the first dude's.

Guys. She frowned. She was seriously done with the lot of them. There had been a time when she hadn't been so completely, one hundred percent distrustful of the gender—almost, but not totally. Until Kevin, that is. Pain filled her, and she did her best to keep it from showing. She'd been thoroughly crushed. Nothing in life could be worth risking that kind of hurt again.

She pushed off with her poles, bending her knees and leaning forward to make the most of the slope's quick descent. Yep, she was totally done with romance and glad of it, too. Icy wind breezed against her face. She loved the speed and the freedom. Snow spewed from her edges as she worked to keep her skis parallel and together.

Talk about exhilarating. The sky, woolly with gray-white clouds stretched out overhead. This was *so* much better than spending the afternoon studying in the library. Knees bent, she absorbed the shock of the groomed run, tucking her poles and preparing for the first curve. The snow was fast!

Echoing sounds of another round of "banzai" rang through the mountain stillness. They were probably mowing down everyone on the run. Not that she was bitter, but who knew what was going through men's heads? She pulled out from the curve, her view limited by trees on one side and the cut slope of the mountain-side on the other. Suddenly a gawky teenaged kid, who must have been taking a break at the side, chose that moment to slide directly into her path.

"Hey, watch out!" She swished to one side, hoping he would go the other way, but did he? No. He panicked, his skis splayed and he wiped out directly in front of her.

Impending disaster. She poled hard, twisting toward the tree line. Her tip hit the loose snow. The shock rattled through the ski and up her right leg. She fought to stay up, but her other tip caught, her bindings gave and she tumbled headfirst through the air. One pole went flying as she threw her hands up to break her fall. She hit hard. Icy cold snow slapped her face. Pain exploded up her right leg as she stopped, stomach down in the snow.

"That hurt." The boy was struggling to get up. "You shouldn't have been going so fast."

"Too fast?" She thought of the banzai guys. They had been speeding. *She* had been going at a sensible pace. As she struggled to turn over, sharp pain carved up her calf. She studied the kid covered with chunks of snow. "Are you all right?"

"I think so. My wrist hurts a little and my face is real cold." He picked himself up, rubbed the ice chunks off his chin and handed her one of her lost poles. "You should be more careful, lady."

"Me?" She pushed up, managing to sit. Her ankle really hurt. Numbly she took the pole. "I think I—"

That was as far as she got. He turned his back and pushed inexpertly off. He was leaving her. She blinked, not quite believing her eyes as he glided away with his brown coat plastered with snow and blond curls corkscrewing out from beneath his russet knit cap. He skidded sideways around the next bend, leaning heavily on his poles and disappeared from her sight, leaving her sprawled out in the snow.

Great. She took a deep breath, hoping that would make the pain go away. It didn't. She looked around for her skis. One was stuck in the snow, and the other was nowhere in sight. It had probably slid off into the trees and she'd never find it.

Now what? She looked up at the sky, gray and cottony. A snowflake hit her in the eye. Double great. She blinked against the discomfort, realizing that she had no way to get down the mountain—she couldn't move her right foot and it had started to snow. Since she'd left her cell phone in her SUV, she had to wait until another skier came around the corner and prayed that it wouldn't be someone who would keep on going.

Lord, please tell me this isn't punishment for blowing off my research paper. She stared up at the steep mountain peaks spearing into the clouds. She sensed no answer on the wind, just the icy cold seeping through her layers of clothing. She couldn't argue. If she had been in the library where she should have been, she wouldn't be hoping her ankle was badly sprained and not broken.

This was just her luck. While she wasn't a study-aholic, she was the kind of girl who always did what she was supposed to do. And why? Because the one time she was hurrying to an appointment and went four miles an hour over the speed limit, she got a ticket. The one time she skipped chemistry class in high school, she got caught. And now she had another story to add to those. The one time she didn't get her research done for her paper, she got stranded in a snow bank. Something to remember the next time she wanted to play instead of study.

Snow pelted her with blizzard force. Great. It was like a sign from heaven agreeing with her. She shivered harder. Now her insides were getting cold. That couldn't be a good sign. Maybe she could somehow ski down the rest of the run or at least far enough down to flag help? A little doubtful, but it was worth a try. She got halfway onto her good foot and saw spots in front of her eyes.

Maybe a better idea was to sit back down. She dropped into the snow, gasping for breath. Surely someone would be coming around the corner any second. She would just have to wait it out. The waiting started to feel like forever.

"Banzai!" The shout echoed from the slope above, sounding like a cry of glory and bravado.

Oh, no. Not the banzai boys. She rolled her eyes, trying to picture the carefree speed lovers taking time to stop and help her. Nope, she couldn't picture it. All she could imagine was them flying by, first in a blur of black and then one of red. A girl couldn't count on guys like that. She'd learned that the hard way. Her father had been the same.

Sure enough, her next glimpse of the banzai guys was a smudge of black zipping around the corner. Veiled by the now-heavy snowfall, it was tough to make out anything more. While she may have imagined it, that smudge seemed to stop moving.

"Whoa. What have we here?" a buttery-warm baritone belted out in surprise. "We have a man down."

A face appeared through the curtain of snow. She could make out a granite hard face and intense, shadowed eyes. He was really tall. With those broad shoulders, he looked just like a linebacker.

"No, correct that. A very pretty girl." He had a kind smile, one that made his eyes crinkle slightly in the corners.

She still couldn't believe that he'd stopped, but she

could believe he was a charmer. Wasn't that just her luck? "You wouldn't happen to have a cell phone, would you?"

"Not on me. Looks like you took a bad spill." To her surprise he stabbed his poles into the snow and hunkered down beside her. He whipped his gloves off and studied her eyes. "Did you hit your head at all when you fell?"

"Mostly my face." Her skin felt red from the snow burn and the freezing temperature. "My head's okay."

"Your pupils are good. Wiggle your fingers for me."

"I'm not that hurt." He was all business, and that *so* did not impress her. "It's my ankle, nothing else."

"Humor me." He took her hands in his, gloves and all, looking every inch like Prince Charming come with a glass slipper.

Good thing she was smart enough to know better. And if her raw heart squeezed with painful memories, she did her best to ignore that. "My left foot is fine. See? I can move it. It's my other ankle."

"No movement at all?" He glanced over his shoulder, holding up one hand. "Hawk, hold up. We've got a casualty."

A red smudge through the snowfall became another wide-shouldered guy with a serious face. "I'll fetch the ski patrol."

"Oh, I really don't want that." That was a lot more fuss and spectacle than she felt comfortable with. "My ankle is probably just sprained. I can make it down to the lodge if I had my other ski."

"I'll look for it." The red-coated guy took off, disappearing into the snowfall.

"He's got eagle eyes, that's why we call him Hawk.

Now, let's get you taken care of. I bet you're pretty cold." He unzipped his jacket. "I'm Pierce Granger."

He looked like a Pierce. Dark haired and teeth-achingly handsome, he was total male confidence. He shrugged out of his jacket. "And you are?"

"Lexie."

"You're going to be all right, Lexie. We'll get you down the slope one way or another, don't worry." He might look like a charmer and was probably the black sheep of his family. But his voice had a steady, reliable quality to it. Not that she wanted to notice.

"Here, we need to keep you warm." He held his jacket in both capable hands.

Before she could reach out to take it, he leaned forward and helped her into it. Her heart skipped four beats. His nearness was like the mountains, strong and incredible, completely out of the ordinary.

Not that she should be noticing that, either. She slipped her arms into the sleeves and told herself not to feel a thing as he settled the garment over her shoulders and against her neck. With her back to him, she could sense the faint flutter of his breath warm against her nape. She shivered, not from the cold but from something deeper.

He was too close. Every instinct she had shouted at her to scoot away, but did she listen? No. She would have looked ridiculous. He was only helping her into his much larger coat like a gentleman.

Not that there were any gentlemen left these days. The weight of the garment settled around her shoulders and she was glad when he put a little distance between them. "Thanks."

"Sure. I'm going to stabilize your ankle so it doesn't

move around too much and cause further injury." He unwound his black scarf and rose, angling his skis away from her. "Don't move. I'll be right back."

"I wasn't planning on racing down the mountain."

"Funny." He liked a girl with a sense of humor. He kicked away, squinting against the torrential snowfall. Flakes pecked at him like sand as he spotted a nearby Douglas fir. A few quick flicks of his wrist and he had some twigs that ought to work. Where had Hawk gotten off to?

He caught a faint spot of red farther down the run. With any luck, his buddy had found the girl's ski and they could assist her down the slope. With the storm worsening, the mountainside would be clearing off. Most folks would rather wait it out in the warm lodge with a steaming cup of something hot. Why wasn't he that smart?

Shivering, he returned to the girl—Lexie. She looked like a Lexie, contemporary and sleek with long, straight black hair. Her white winter gear was classic and up-scale. Even pale with pain, she was striking. She had a heart-shaped face with big, expressive blue eyes and a cute, sloping nose. Her delicate chin could have been carved out of ivory.

Not that beauty affected a hard man like him. "Where do you hail from?"

"Wyoming, for the most part."

"No kidding. Me, too. Grew up near Buffalo."

"I have family not too far from there, near Swinging Rope." Affection warmed her words.

She must have a great family. He stripped the needles from the small branches. "What are you doing in Montana, besides skiing?"

"Going to school. I'm a grad student at MCU."

"Montana Christian University. My sister goes there." It was a coincidence, he told himself as he gently secured her injury. "You wouldn't happen to know Giselle Granger?"

"Giselle is on my floor." Sometimes it was a very small world. "She's told me a little about her family. Not much. She's a fairly private person. You wouldn't be the brother who can't hold a job?"

"Not me. I've been working for the same outfit for the past eight years." He tied the last knot and checked the splinting. It would hold. "I'm going back for another four."

"You're the brother in the Army?"

"Hey, you don't have to look so surprised. And why did you automatically assume I was the derelict of the family?"

"First impressions. I saw you shoot down the mountain on your earlier run."

"Two weeks ago I was belly down in a sand dune being shot at. I was just letting off steam and really glad to be here." He pushed against the snow, sliding forward. "I'm actually a rather responsible guy."

"Really?" She didn't look as if she believed him, although she got prettier the more he looked at her. Snowflakes sifted over her like poetry as she took a shaky breath. "What do you do in the Army? I don't think your sister ever said."

"I'm surprised she mentioned me at all."

"She's mentioned you in passing. I'm her resident advisor."

"Sure, she's mentioned her R.A. I got the image of someone much older. You can't be what, twenty-one, twenty-two?"

"Twenty three. How about you?" She was watching him intently, as if she were trying to figure him out.

Good luck with that. He tried to do it every day and hadn't nailed it yet. "I'm twenty-six. Right now, I'm on leave."

"You're not answering my first question."

"That would be true." He thought of Giselle's letters and how she had begged him to get out at the end of his contract. Well, here he was, at the end of his contract and he knew what he was going to be up against. His family thought he'd done enough, that he was playing a dangerous game of chance with his life.

If they only knew the half of it, they would never say it. They would never ask him to give up his goals, his principles and his beliefs for his own safety. Lexie hadn't figured out what he was yet, and he said the words, not knowing how she would react. "I'm an Army Ranger."

"Oh." She took a step back. "Special Forces."

He'd seen this before. A lot of well-meaning people heard those words and equated it with something bad. It was hard enough to do the job of fighting for this country, harder still to keep his armor up and his defenses in place on the home front. Someone had to do the tough, careful and protective job of keeping America safe from hatred and evil. He had seen countries where people were not safe in their homes from conscience-less, well-armed militias. The thought of that happening to his country broke his heart.

Hawk skied up. "I didn't find anything. Do you want me to fetch someone, or should we take her down with us?"

"I'll take her." He couldn't explain why he felt protective of her. "If that's all right with you, Lexie."

"Please. The last thing I want is to be hauled off the run in a bright red sled-stretcher thing in front of everyone. I'd be embarrassed."

He understood. He liked the way she blushed at the idea of all that attention. He'd been away too long. He had forgotten there was good in this world. He knelt to take her hand. "I'm going to carry you on my back. Ready?"

"As ready as I'll ever be. I'm messing up your fun. You came here to ski, not to take care of me."

"Do you hear me complaining? Besides, I like to be useful. It keeps up my self-esteem."

"As if you need any help with that."

"Hey, you're right." He kept his tone light.

She managed an almost-smile until her gaze shifted to the slope of the mountain ahead, shrouded in snowfall. She must be thinking of the trip to come. Her eyes squinted against the pain and her dainty chin set with determination. A nice girl with strength. That was an interesting combination. He kept his emotional armor in place as he gently helped her over his shoulder. He'd carried men before, but they had been soldiers. It had been nothing like this, with her a light burden he could not forget. Her sweet scent of lilacs made him aware that some things in life were too good for a man like him.

He rose slowly, testing his balance, adjusting to her weight. "Don't worry. I won't go too fast."

"I wasn't worried."

"Good. Does that mean you have a little faith in me?"

"Maybe just a little." Her voice was thin and shaky, as if she was in a lot more pain than she cared to admit.

He knew what that was like, too. He wanted to pretend it was no big deal that he felt out of place here in this country he fought so hard to protect. But he did. He'd been gone so long, he felt like a stranger to himself. He could no longer see the man he used to be. He *had* to think that the man he'd become was much better.

He wasn't sure. For now, he guessed it didn't matter. Getting the woman help was his only mission. He braced his knees against the added weight, took the poles Hawk handed him, dug in and pushed off. The snowfall closed in around them, cutting off all view of the outside world.

She'd never been so miserable in her life. When the faint blur of the lodge's lights broke through the storm, Lexie nearly cried with relief. The cold and pain were at an end. She hungered for the warmth of the lodge like a starving woman for food. Every time Pierce moved, sharp pain pared through her foot and shin bone. All she wanted was to collapse in front of the fire crackling in one of the lodge's huge, old-fashioned stone hearths, cradle a cup of steaming chamomile tea in both hands and never move her ankle again.

Only a bit farther, she told herself. She had to hold on a little longer, that was all.

"We're almost there." Pierce's steady tone reassured her. He had borne her weight all the way down the mountain and he was still going, alone because he had sent his friend ahead to check if there was a medical center at the lodge.

She didn't know, but she was praying for it. She didn't have a clue how she was going to drive on compact snow and ice all the way to the hospital in town. It was starting to get dark. That meant she should be heading for home. She was working the late shift, although how she was going to do that with a broken ankle was anyone's guess.

This was definitely the last time she was playing hooky. Next time she had the urge to play instead of finish her work, she was going to toss that idea right out the window. God must have been watching out for her, because of all the people who could have come down that mountain to help her, Pierce was the best choice. Who else could have slung her over his shoulder and skied down an advanced run? He'd made the trip as easy as he could on her, moving sparingly, checking to make sure she was holding on all right, and now, lifting her gently to the ground. She was aware of another pair of hands taking her other elbow. Hawk must have come back from the lodge.

"They'll take care of you here," he was saying.

There was an outside entrance to the medical center, she saw now. It was nothing more than a comfortable-looking room on the bottom floor of the lodge set up with a waiting area and, beyond another open door, a small examining room. "They mostly send the serious stuff by ambulance or airlift into the city, but Hawk thinks they can set it for you here if it's not too bad. Do you need me to call anyone?"

"I came up here on my own." She hopped two feet to the chair by the door and slumped into it. She quaked from cold and pain, and she hated that it showed. It was too vulnerable.

"You're not alone." His words came quietly.

She read the sincere caring in his eyes. Somehow that honest concern scared her more than anything ever had.

"Thank you." Her voice sounded strained and unnatural, and clearing her throat didn't fix it. "I appreciate all that you've done for me."

"No problem. Here's the nurse practitioner now." He nodded toward the inside door, where a stern-looking woman with a short cap of dark hair and a white coat studied her intently.

"See you around, gorgeous." He winked, flashed his amazing smile. He took two steps into the veil of snow and wind and disappeared from her sight.

Chapter Two

"Lexie."

Balancing on her new pair of crutches wasn't easy, but she managed to look up at the sound of her name without toppling over. "Pierce?"

"Yep, it's me."

She couldn't believe her eyes. Paper cup in hand, he really was standing in the middle of the nearly vacant corridor. At the sight of him, gladness rose like a bubble within her. She ignored it. "I didn't think I would see you again. I have your coat and scarf."

"I know. I was coming back to check on you."

"You were?" She stopped, leaned one crutch against the wall and, balancing awkwardly, untied his jacket from around her waist. "That's beyond the call of duty."

"I'm big on duty." He winked, all charm, but she wasn't fooled. There were shadows in his eyes and steel in his voice. He wasn't as carefree as he'd first seemed. He took the coat, bunching it up in one hand. "Thanks. How are you getting back home?"

"I've got it figured out, don't you worry." She might

not have the best plan or the least expensive one, but it would do. She wasn't good at leaning on other people, even worse at asking for what she needed. She thought of her friends back on campus and any number of the freshmen kids on her floor with cars. Surely one of them would come to fetch her if she called. The trouble was, she couldn't make herself do it. "You don't have to hang around. I appreciate it, but I know you have better things to do."

"What would that be?" He rescued the lone crutch from the wall and held it for her.

"Flying down the advanced run, for one thing. Didn't you say this was your first fun run in a long time?" She settled onto both crutches and took another wobbly step. He really didn't have to be so nice. "You should be out enjoying yourself."

"Who says I'm not?" There was something patient in the way he slowed down, keeping pace with her. Something pleasant about him that reminded her of being carried down the mountain over his iron-strong shoulders. He looked even more invincible in the bright light as he came closer. "Besides, if I went back out, I wouldn't enjoy myself knowing you're on crutches. You've got to be hurting."

"I'm trying not to think about it." She wasn't glad he'd come to check on her—at least that's what she told herself. "You were pretty great up on that mountain. Something tells me that I'm not the first casualty you've come across."

"Not even close." He swallowed, as if battling down something he didn't want to speak of. "But if I say you are the prettiest, you are going to think I'm trying to pick you up."

"True."

"And then you're going to send me packing. You don't entirely like me."

"I'm not looking to be picked up."

"I'm not a picker upper. No way. Not me. I'm a loner." They reached the end of the hall and he hit the elevator button. "I used to fight it. I used to think I could change, but I was wrong."

"I've been wrong before, too."

"I'm not a man used to failure, but it's one limit I've had to face. Love is one battlefield I want to stay off of."

"So do I." Sadness passed briefly over her face, as if she knew how he felt. "I thought I had finally found an honest, trustworthy man, but he was the exact opposite. Who needs that kind of trouble?"

"I'm in complete agreement." The elevator dinged and he waited for the doors to open. His heart was heavy. He tried not to think of his failures. "What happened with the guy?"

"Kevin. He was a prelaw student. We were in the same senior philosophy course. Ethics."

The doors opened and he held them, waiting for her to hobble into the car. "Let me guess. It was ironic."

"Exactly. He started talking to me before class. I invited him to the Bible study we were starting in my dorm. He came across as this completely nice guy with great values." Exhaustion bruised the delicate skin beneath her eyes. She fell silent, as if hurt and embarrassed to go on.

"And he tried playing you."

"How did you know?" She leaned against the back wall, gazing up at him with those fabulous eyes.

"I've seen it before and before you wonder, I'm not

one of those types of men." He hit the lobby button. "Kevin was the perfect boyfriend for the first few months, right?"

"Right. He made me believe—" She stared down at the floor. Her dark hair fell in a sleek curtain around her face, shielding her emotion from him. "He told me that he'd fallen deeply in love with me."

"And so you fell in love with him."

"Yes, and that makes me feel really stupid now. I never should have trusted him." She looked down, as if trying to hide what had hurt. "He did everything right. He was especially supportive of my wanting an advanced degree. Some men think a woman they love should be content to be dependent on them, so I really liked that about him."

"I understand. Women have dreams, too. My mom gave up hers to follow my dad from base to base. When he went AWOL on her, she had four of us to support. She would have had an easier time if she had training or an education to fall back on."

"That's what happened to my mom, too." She stared at him, understanding what he hadn't said. That when his dad ran out on his mom, he had run out on him, too. She knew, because she'd never been able to resolve her dad's abandonment. Accept it, yes. Patch up their relationship, yes. But deep down, it would always be a scarred-over wound. "Kevin waited until I trusted him completely. Until I was head over heels in love with him. That's when he started pressuring me for, well, you know. I'm not that kind of girl, so he had to go."

"I'm sorry. I know how that can feel, to fall for someone and have them turn the tables on you. It happened to me, too. Different circumstance, different story, same outcome."

The elevator dinged again. The doors opened to the bright main floor packed with skiers taking refuge from the storm. He waited, letting her go first, making sure the doors didn't close on her as she ambled out into the fray. There was movement everywhere, people going from the sitting areas to the shops, folks coming in from the slopes coated with snow, and conversation roaring like a tank engine.

He spotted a couple of places in front of the fire and pointed them out. "That looks like a good place to park. You're looking pretty pale. Something tells me you might want to get that foot elevated."

"You could be right." He liked the way she tried to smile, even when she had to be hurting. That showed spunk.

The smart thing to do would be to keep his distance, to help her out, but not be affected by it. The soldier in him did it all the time. The man in him couldn't bring himself to do it. Maybe because they had walked a common path. He knew what it felt like to fall in love with someone and then discover they were someone else. That kind of deception was brutal.

"What happened to you?" She inched forward. "Wait, you aren't going to tell me. You are the type of guy to keep your heartache where no one can see it."

"True." He kept at her side. He liked the way she crutched forward doggedly, although the stone floor had to be tough going.

"That's it? You're really not going to tell me."

"There's not much to tell." He waited while she crept around the overstuffed chair before he took her crutches from her. "I thought Cindy would be supportive of my career, but she wasn't."

"Do you mean she was worried about you? Or that she wanted you to be something you weren't?" She eased into the chair slowly, watching him with her wise eyes.

It was like taking a blow to the chest. She understood. He wanted to argue it away or deny it, but no one—not Cindy, not his family, nor even his buddies—could see what had wounded him. Why he'd ended their engagement.

"That's it exactly." He leaned the crutches against the wall. The heat of the fire blasted him as he crossed to the chair beside her. "She knew that I wanted a long Army career. She knew it came with a lot of sacrifice and time spent apart. But as soon as she got the ring on her finger, she started needing more than I could give her and found someone who could. She left me—" He stopped short of saying the words.

But she knew them. "For another guy?"

"Bingo." He stared into the fire. "She said the Army didn't pay enough. That I wasn't enough."

"She actually told you that?"

"Oh, yeah. And I had been the fool who loved her."

"Then she hadn't loved you, not if she could leave you." Lexie winced as she lifted her foot onto the ottoman. Pierce leaned forward with a pillow and placed it under her cast. He had a gentle touch. With the firelight on his face, he looked harsh as raw steel. She relaxed into the chair. "I don't know about you, but I felt pretty dumb."

"Yep. Like I've been taken for a ride. But the truth is, I wasn't around enough. She had a point." He handed her the cup he'd been carrying. "This is for you. I figured a hot cup of tea would make you feel better. It's chamomile."

"Chamomile?" She stared at him in shock. How had he known? With the warmth from the fire, the comfort of the chair, the heat from the cup seeping into her hands, it was the very image that had kept her going through the pain and cold on the ride down the mountain.

"I can get you something else if you want," he offered.

"No, this is perfect. Thanks. Where's your friend?"

"Hawk is out clearing off and warming up my rental truck. You're going to need a ride home."

"Oh, I've got it covered." She took a sip of the steaming brew. The steamy, herbal goodness warmed her all the way down. She felt better. Infinitely better.

"I'm afraid that means you're going to try to drive with your left foot. I don't think that's a good idea."

"Neither do I." Why wasn't she going to confess her plan to him? Because she knew deep down he would point out all its flaws, and there were many. She took another sip, hoping inspiration would strike. She couldn't think of another solution, at least one that didn't depend on someone else.

"Maybe I should make sure you get home."

"Why are you doing all this?"

"You're my sister's R.A. Isn't that enough of a reason?"

"But you don't know me. I don't know you. I'm grateful, don't get me wrong, but you've gone beyond all duty. I don't want to trouble you anymore."

"That's a strategic and polite way of saying that you don't want to be beholden to me. I help you and then who knows what I'll expect?"

"Something like that."

"I've known people like that, too. No worries." He leaned closer, the perfect image of intense male honor. "Give me your keys. I'll warm up your car and bring it up to the curb. I'll drive you home, and Hawk can tail us. And don't worry, no strings attached."

"But that means you'll miss your chance to ski."

"Maybe we'll come back for night skiing. It's no biggie." He rose, towering over her, his jaw set, his eyes determined and a grin flirting at the corners of his mouth. "It's not like I'm a complete stranger since you know my sister, so I'm not taking no for an answer. Get used to it."

Why that made her want to laugh, she couldn't say. "I don't like domineering guys."

"See? That's your insurance I have no ulterior motive. It's not like I can charm you." He flashed her a hint of a smile and while it was only for a moment, it was long enough for her to see the goodness in him. His smile was calm and steady and kind.

She sighed all the way to her soul. She had a weakness for kind, big strong men. Any moment now her untrustworthy guy-meter was going to go off like a smoke alarm, but there was no *ding! ding!* like a warning bell. No instinctive urge to escape the man. No looming sense of impending doom.

"What's your vehicle and where are you parked?" he asked, shoulders braced, as if ready for his mission.

Yep, she definitely had to keep her defenses up with this one.

Snow hammered his face as he swept Lexie into his arms. Hawk took her crutches and disappeared through the storm. White-out conditions, a heady wind and the snow was deep powder beneath his boots. Perfect skiing conditions. Some folks would pack it in and head home, but everything in him ached to catch a ride on the chair lift and hit the slope as hard and as fast as he could go.

Maybe next time. He feared by the time he'd gotten Lexie back to her dorm and made it back up the mountain, they would probably have closed the runs. As it was, they would be lucky if the state patrol didn't close the pass. Well, they'd cross that bridge if they got to it.

In the meantime, her weight in his arms was sweetness. Not something he was used to feeling. A light shone out of the stormy shadows—the dome light. Hawk had the passenger door open, the crutches stowed, and the backseat ready for the patient. He told himself he was more than glad to lower her gently into the shelter of the vehicle. Snow no longer stung his face, although it did beat an angry rhythm against his back as he leaned over to help buckle her up. Her hair brushing against his chin felt like the finest strands of silk. His arms felt strangely empty as he took a step away.

"All settled?" he asked, his voice unusually husky.

"Very. Thanks." Her grateful smile was pure wholesome charm. "Tell me you don't drive the way you ski."

"If I do, then what's wrong with that?" he quipped. She was teasing him. Well, he could do it, too. "Buckle up. I suggest you hold on to something."

"Funny. I feel so much better now." She collapsed against the seat, exhaustion bruising her face. "My chauffeur is a comedian."

"Only an amateur comedian, but a good snow driver." He closed the door, welcoming the numbing cold of the icy snow. It whipped his face, driving out the warmer emotions that had taken root in his chest. He had given up on love. It didn't exist for him. He wasn't good at it. He had no business feeling anything tender toward anyone. End of story.

Besides, a girl like Lexie would never want anything to do with a man like him.

"You okay?" Hawk asked, rattling his keys in one hand.

"I'm good." There were some things best left unsaid. "What's the latest on the roads?"

"Word is the pass is about to close."

"Let's hope this isn't going to be a short ride." He waved his buddy off, who headed for the truck parked behind Lexie's SUV. Snow had already accumulated on the side window, so he scrubbed it off with his sleeve before he dropped behind the wheel.

It was going to be interesting. The wipers on high were not keeping up with the snow. He buckled in, his gaze straying to the rearview mirror, where she was right there in plain sight. Her dark hair was slightly mussed and dappled with melting snow. His heart began to beat faster as he put the rig in gear and put in a prayer for a safe trip. He hoped the pass would be open when they hit it or they would all be stuck at the lodge for a good while.

"Is this your first time rescuing a skier, or is this how all your days off go?"

"My days off are far and few between. Even now, I could be called in." He released the e-brake and eased away from the curb. "I have packed injured soldiers on my back before, just not on skis."

"Giselle has only mentioned you in passing, but I know she worries about what you do. If you're an Army Ranger, you get into a lot of danger."

"Now and then." Most of the time, but that was harder to say. He figured a girl as sheltered and as sweet as Lexie might not want to hear about the details he could tell her. "It's a dangerous world, and the military keeps me pretty busy."

"You've been deployed for a long time. Am I remembering right?"

"It started to feel like a decade." He circled through the lot, squinting hard for the signs that ought to point him in the direction of the highway. There they were, coated with snow. He couldn't read them, but he knew he was on the right track. In the vehicle behind them, he could just make out the flash signal of Hawk's truck.

He took the on-ramp at a crawl. If any cars were on the road ahead of him, he saw no evidence of them. The windshield wipers beat a quick cadence. The defroster blasted air on high. "You know when you watch a movie that's set ten years ago, and you realize how everything used to be?"

"I do. How funny the clothes back then were, when they didn't seem funny at the time. And hairstyles."

"That's how I feel a lot of the time. I come back from a forward base in the desert and suddenly I can order pizza with cheesy sticks."

"I love cheesy sticks."

"And there's more channels than I can count on the TV. There's TiVo and call waiting and people rushing around in their cars without worrying about mortar fire. It's great, don't get me wrong, just surreal. At first. Until I acclimate, which is just about the time I ship out again."

"You probably get used to living a pretty sparse existence when you're deployed. One of my friends, we used to room together, she married a marine. He did recon, and it sounded as if his life was duty, training and missions."

"That about sums it up. Free time can be ten minutes a day. Other days, that's just wishful thinking."

"And you had an entire afternoon off and I messed it up."

"You did." His eyes twinkled at her in the mirror. "Because you were a bad skier, here I am."

"Hey! I'm not a bad skier. It wasn't me. Exactly." She liked that he was laughing; it was a cozy, friendly sound. "There was this teenager. He got in front of me and wiped out. I couldn't get around him in time."

"I remember that kid. He was hanging out off the side, scratching his head, like he'd decided to take the harder run, gotten around the first turn and realized he'd made a mistake."

"That's the one. I'm glad he wasn't really hurt, but I could have done without the broken ankle. I have to work tonight. I hate to think about what my boss is going to say."

"You can still be a resident advisor, right?" He peered straight ahead, concentrating on navigating the dark, snowbound road. "You aren't lifting heavy boxes or operating big machinery."

"No, I have a second job. At the library."

"Two jobs?"

"Graduate tuition at a private university is way expensive. I went to a state university for my B.A., but bad memories." She could only see part of his face reflected in the rearview mirror. His frown of concentration was interrupted by surprise.

"Kevin went to the same university?"

"Bingo. My mom isn't exactly happy about it. She thinks I have a better chance of finding a husband at one of the larger universities."

"A husband? I thought you weren't looking." His gaze met hers for a brief moment.

Her heart ached at the hard flash of distrust. Like her, it came naturally these days. The feeling that you could be tricked all over again. "I'm not looking, no, but my mom is hopeful. She loved Kevin."

"Did she think he was the right guy?"

"Uh, yeah. He came from a good family, not a well-off one, but respectable. He met her on parents' weekend and charmed her, too."

"What pick-up line did he use on you?"

Lexie watched the corners of his eyes crinkle just a little, as if he knew he was right on target. Okay, so she had been a little defensive about pick-up lines. "He told me his heart stopped beating the first time he saw my face."

"Isn't that from a song or something?"

"At the time I was too charmed to notice how shallow it was. He flashed his dimples at me and he was so attentive. He did everything right." She remembered how whole her heart had been, how hard she had searched for the right guy. How had she made such a mistake? She had wanted to believe, for one thing, and he had done his best to make her believe. "But I think everything has worked out for the best. I'm happy at MCU."

"But you're working two jobs."

"I don't mind. A little hard work never hurt anyone, at least that's what they say. But my mom—" She was talking too much. Revealing far more than she wanted to. Maybe it was the pain medication. Or maybe it was easier to talk to someone whom she would never see again. "I really disappointed her that I moved so far away. I'm gone all the time now. I'm sorry, you probably don't want to hear this."

"Hey, I understand more than you know. I'm the biggest disappointment to my folks in family history." He paused as flares alongside the road narrowed the three lanes to one. He hit the turn signal and eased to a stop behind a semi. "Sometimes you just have to take the hit and stick with your course. It isn't easy, but nothing worthwhile ever is."

"Exactly. I have to find my own way, that's part of growing into the person you're going to be." Listening to the swipe of the wipers and the crunch of the tires in the snow, she thought how strange it was to be with a guy she had so much in common with. "Why are you a disappointment to your parents? Aren't they proud of what you do?"

"That's a loaded question. You know what I do, right?"

"You protect this country."

"I do a very small part, but it's mine to do." He fell silent for a moment as they crept past the state patrol's barricade, where one lane was still open. As far as she could see the road was single file, with red taillights twinkling faintly in the furiously falling snow.

Finally he spoke. "I do what is necessary. My stepfather thinks it's wrong to carry a gun and use it. My mother thinks I'll turn violent, like my dad ended up doing. My sister thinks I'm going to get killed, so I should get out while I'm still breathing. And since my younger brother was killed last year on a mission, everyone pretty much agrees with her."

"I'm sorry. I didn't know about your brother." She

thought of Giselle, the sweet freshman girl who didn't know what to major in, who missed her mom so much it hurt, who loved Bible study and knitting with her friends in the lounge. She remembered how Giselle had worried about one brother in the military. Lexie hadn't known she'd lost another.

It is amazing how deep we can bury our deepest hurts, she thought, aching for the girl and for the stoic man in the front seat. She never would have guessed the guy shouting "banzai" harbored a deep loss. She thought about how much time she spent glancing along the surface of her life and of others. It was the layers that mattered and what was hidden beneath. Those were the things so hard to see at first glance, and sometimes at all.

"Was your brother a Ranger like you?"

"Yep. He died in my arms." His voice sounded hollow, like the spent casing of a fired bullet. He said no more as the twilight became night and the drive off the mountain more treacherous.

He didn't have to. She could feel his sorrow as if it were her own.

Chapter Three

"This is it." The SUV's headlamps spotlighted the sign tucked in an arrangement of carefully clipped hedges. "Whitman Hall."

This was the end of the line. Mission over. He'd gotten Lexie's prescription at the pharmacy and delivered her here, safe and sound. The snow beat at them with blizzard force, but they had made it. He peered up at what he could see of the dormitory through the storm—red brick and yellow rectangles of windows shining against the dark. "What's your floor?"

"Four." She paused over the click of a seat belt releasing. "The top floor."

"Maybe I had better see you up—or as far as they let guys go. You might need help."

"There's an elevator just inside the door. I'll be fine."

"Sure you will." He unlatched his belt and shoved open the door. "But I'm helping you inside anyway. Hawk can park this for you in the lot. What do you want me to do with the key?"

"You can leave it at the security desk. It's just inside

the front door." She'd already hopped out of the vehicle and was balancing on her good foot. "I'm not sure how well snow and crutches are going to mix."

"You don't have to worry about it tonight." He gently took her hand, steadied her and lifted her into his arms. She was light and little, hardly a burden at all. If a small spark of tenderness flickered in his chest, he ignored it. He wasn't that kind of man. "I'll see you to the door. Got a hold of your crutches?"

"Yes. Oops." Her grip must have slipped because something bonked his right shin bone. "Sorry about that."

"I'm tough. I can handle it." That made her almost smile. The spark flickered again. He tamped it down. Leaving the vehicle running, he marched through the knee-deep snow. The pathway up to the grand entrance was well lit, which made the going easy. "Are you sure there isn't anything else I can get you?"

"As if you haven't done enough. I'll be fine."

"It's dinnertime. What about the dining hall? Are you going to manage all right?"

"I'll figure it out." She watched him with her wide blue eyes intently, as if she were trying to see beneath the layers.

That was no place for her. He shouldered open the heavy glass door, taking care with her. "I'll give my sister a call. There's got to be a house phone here somewhere, right? She can come down and get a tray for you."

"Are you always like this?"

"Like what? In charge, you mean?" He carried her past the security desk.

"No, I mean bossy." Not that she minded. She was

quite able to handle a strong-minded man. "I can take it from here, Pierce."

"You're independent. I like that."

"I don't like leaning on other people. I don't know if that's independent or just a sign I need therapy."

His laughter rumbled like thunder, and she didn't want to like the sound or hear more of it. She savored one last moment in his arms, feeling his strength and capability. She felt humbled by him and somehow sad as he eased her down gently. She put her weight on her good foot and held his arm while he helped her straighten out her crutches.

He was like a mountain. She sensed his honor and his integrity, the truths he hid beneath his quick grin and charming dimples.

"I guess this is goodbye for now, Lexie Evans." His hazel eyes warmed, revealing flecks of forest-green and pure gold. "Maybe I'll see you again."

"Maybe." It felt more like a promise as she watched him stride away with his shoulders unerringly straight and strong, strangely unreal, as if untouched by the life around him.

College girls trailed in from the library or social events, flocked with snow, and their conversations punctuated with laughter. The security team—mostly male students—stood around, talking basketball with measured excitement. The scent of pot roast and baking bread wafted from the dining hall, where flatware clinked against stoneware and rang like a thousand bells.

Pierce did not seem a part of it. He was an island unto himself as he strolled out the door. The snowfall and the night stole him from her sight.

But not from her thoughts. No, there was no chance of that.

"Lexie!" Amber McKaslin, one of her freshmen girls, skidded to a stop, a cup of soda in hand. "What happened to you? Are you okay?"

"I'm perfect, except for the ankle I banged up just a little when I was skiing." It would heal soon enough. "Are you on your way upstairs?"

"Yeah, a bunch of us are going to watch a movie. Do you want to come?"

"Thanks, but I'm going to get something to eat." Her injury was starting to throb worse, in rhythmic, sharp beats. She would ask one of the kitchen workers to pack a to-go carton for her. "Maybe I'll drop by later."

"Yeah, then you can see the sweater I've started. I've got the prettiest yarn." Amber started walking backward and stopped. "Maybe I'd better come carry stuff for you."

"That's nice. Thanks." She positioned her weight on her crutches and moved forward. Already she was back to her normal life, but it no longer felt the same. She glanced over her shoulder, knowing that Pierce was long gone but still, something within her looked for him.

"At least we got some skiing in." There was a thunk as Hawk closed the hotel door. The hotel's latch clanked in the echoing room. "There's always tomorrow."

"For you." Pierce dropped the food bags on the small round table by the window. His room was modest, but serviceable. "Giselle has my day packed."

"Then you're out of luck." Hawk set down the drinks—extrathick chocolate shakes. "I'm hitting the slopes tomorrow. I report on Monday. I'm getting in what fun I can."

"I've got nothing but time." He didn't add that once his leave was up and he signed on the dotted line, he would be running from dusk to dawn, too. He decided to enjoy what leisure he had. It was hard earned. He took a seat at the table and hit the remote. The TV flashed to life, and he found a sports show as he dug his burgers out of the bags.

"I've been thinking I might not re-up." Hawk delivered that news as casually as if he'd been discussing whether or not to buy a new pair of boots.

"What do you mean?" Pierce couldn't register it. "You're getting out?"

"Considering it." He looked unaffected, like he didn't care either way.

Pierce wasn't fooled. You didn't get to be a Ranger by not caring deeply about it. "That's a big decision. What will you do if you stay out?"

"Maybe my uncle can get me a job with the forest service back home. Think I'd make a good forest ranger?"

"They don't let you jump out of airplanes."

"That I would miss." Hawk bowed his head in silent prayer.

Pierce did the same. He had a hard time focusing with his buddy's news still ringing in his ears. Quit the Army? Go back to civilian life? Pierce couldn't imagine putting down his weapon or forgoing his commitment to serve.

Lord, please lead my friend down the right path for him. And if You wouldn't mind helping me along on mine, too, I would appreciate it. He thought of Lexie, probably warm and snug in her fourth-floor room, with her foot up. *Please watch over her, too. Thank You for my blessings. Amen.*

"Are you serious about this?" He unwrapped his first burger and took a bite.

"Pretty." Hawk dragged three fries through a puddle of ketchup and munched on them. "It's not the same since we lost Tim."

"Nothing is." They hardly spoke of his loss. Even thinking about his brother made the shrapnel of grief cut deeper into his heart. Carrying Tim's coffin and laying him to rest had been the hardest thing he'd ever done. "I can't say I haven't thought about it, too, but quitting isn't for me."

That was enough said. They both felt it. Talk turned to the game that came on. But something had changed. The personal price for what they did ran high. No argument there. Some days it felt too high. On other days, it was worth every bit it cost and more.

One price was life. He'd lost a few soldiers under his command and comrades he loved like family. He'd lost Tim, who used to trail him everywhere as a little boy, who could climb trees higher than anyone else had the nerve to and who had once loved to play in the creek that meandered along the property line, separating his folks' place from Hawk's family's land. The three of them had been simple country boys, barefoot and running through the fields and forest, playing childish games of make-believe.

Another cost was the life others had. He'd gotten a good dose of that today seeing the campus. It was a cost he thought about long after Hawk had said good-night and left for his room next door. A cost that troubled him in the dark.

He tossed and turned on the mattress, listening to heat fan from the wall unit, unable to forget the image of Lexie Evans, with snow clinging to her jet-black hair, balancing on her crutches in the middle of the dormitory hallway. Life had surrounded her, all that she was experiencing, all that she was learning, and the people she had time to get to know.

There was only room in his life for discipline and service. It was his choice, so why was he thinking of her?

"Let me get a pillow for your foot," Amber was saying as she set Lexie's backpack on the carpet by one of the chairs in their fourth-floor lounge. "I tore up my ankle when I was running track one year, and the two weeks I was on crutches were torture. What else can I fetch for you?"

"I'm fine. Really." Lexie leaned her crutches against the brick wall and eased into the chair. Talk about relief. She'd had a light morning since the earlier classes had been cancelled because of the storm, but she was more exhausted than ever. She put her awkward cast up on the pillow-topped ottoman. "Thanks, Amber. I owe you big-time."

"No, you don't. You've helped me out, like, a million times." The girl flashed a quick smile, gave a finger wave. "I've got to hit the books. I have this killer poetry paper due on Monday."

"Good luck." Lexie reached for the TV remote on the coffee table. Her stomach rumbled, but she hadn't felt up to tackling the cafeteria during the noon rush. She channel-surfed through the movie channels, finally settling on an old favorite. The black-and-white hero was larger than life and entirely heroic. She might not believe in love for herself, but that didn't mean she couldn't enjoy a good romantic movie.

"Do you want us to get you anything, Lexie?" Rose Everly called out.

"I'm good. Thanks." She smiled at sweet, thoughtful Rose, who had a thick volume of Dickens clutched in the crook of her arm. "I'm going down later."

"Okay. Let me know if you need help." She scampered out of sight, her footfalls light on the stairs.

"Room service." A familiar baritone rumbled behind her.

"Pierce?" She squinted over the back of the chair, sure she had to be imagining him. He looked good behind the trays of food he balanced. His short, dark hair was wind-tousled and made darker by the navy blue MCU sweatshirt he wore. "I see you made a stop at the bookstore."

"Yep. If I'm going to spend a day on campus, I'm going to do it right. As an MCU Cougar." He set the trays on the nearby coffee table. The delicious aromas of French dip, fries and apple crisp scented the air as he dropped into the chair next to her. "Giselle and I were standing in line to get swiped at the dining hall and we spotted you going into the elevator. I thought I'd bring you lunch. Figured you might have a hard time on that slick floor. Everyone has tracked in snow, including me."

"That's very gentlemanly of you. I'm totally going to have to change my opinion of you now."

"You mean it wasn't good before this?"

"Of course it was, but it's higher now. That's hard to do." She didn't want to be glad to see him. She shouldn't be pleased that he had thought of her, but she was. "I can't believe your sister let you go. She was practically skipping down the hall this morning because her big brother was coming."

"She's been bouncing all morning. She hauled me to two of her classes. Then wrote notes to me the entire time, and there was no way I could snooze. I had to pay attention."

"Welcome to my world."

"My head is spinning from all the information I couldn't help absorbing. I've always wondered what I missed by not going to college. Now I know. A headache from too much thinking and a backache from packing all those big textbooks around."

"Those are my two biggest problems," she said lightly. "Just as I'm sure that your biggest problems are blisters from marching around in your boots and traveling all over the world."

"Yep, those are my only hardships." He hauled the coffee table between the chairs as a makeshift table. The last thing he wanted to talk about was his work. The weight of it felt like an anvil, heavy, serious and ever present. This campus was a different world from his. This moment, a separate peace. "How's the ankle?"

"How do ya think?" Her eyes were sparkling and the color was back in her face. She apparently didn't want to elaborate. "Will you say grace, or should I?"

"Go for it." He was curious what she would say. Something standard or something cute? She was the cute type, he could see it now, in her boot-cut jeans, which accommodated her cast, and trendy blue sweater, which brought out the deep sapphire color of her eyes.

"Dear Father." She bowed her head. Her black hair tumbled forward to curtain her face. "Please keep us mindful of our blessings and of Your grace in our lives. Bless this food and our new friendship. Amen."

"Amen." He unclasped his hands and nudged one of

the trays closer, so she could reach it more easily. "So, you think we're friends?"

"It's a perilous thought, I know! Any guy who carries me down a mountain is definitely in the friend category. It's automatic. I think it's a state law or something." She daintily unfolded a paper napkin and spread it across her knees.

"It's probably in the state constitution." He could quip, too. "So, you really want to be friends?"

"Maybe you have more friends than you can count, but I cherish every friendship I can get."

He could see that about her. She was friendly and light, but careful somehow. When she spoke to you, it was as if she thought you were important enough to really listen to. As if you had her respect. He liked it. Okay, maybe he just liked her.

But not a lot. He wasn't about to get attached or anything. He couldn't remember the last time he'd really let someone behind his armor. Maybe he never really had.

"I made some buddies in the Army." He took a bite of the sandwich. It was pretty good. Better than the chow he was used to. "You met Hawk. I'm tight with my team of guys."

"I can see that about you." She neatly gathered up her sandwich with both slender hands. "What about your childhood friends? Do you keep in touch with them?"

"I did for a while after I first got in." His chest went cold; there it was again, that feeling that he was out of sync with the world. "My high school buddies and me, we don't have much in common these days. It's been eight years since graduation."

"Don't you go back to visit and see family and friends?"

"Now and then, but I mostly get only short trips. Enough time for a quick family visit and that's it. Then I'm gone again." He took another bite so he wouldn't have to say more.

"You must feel like a world apart. You visit, catch up and disappear for a long time." She studied him thoughtfully as she pushed a slice of roast beef into place between the thick French bread. "Then the next time you visit, everything is different."

"That's it." How she understood, he didn't know. He felt some of the iron around his heart ease a tad. "Two weeks ago I was taking machine-gun fire. Now I'm sitting in a dorm lounge eating lunch with you. In another two weeks, I'll be back in the sandbox. *That's* real life for me. The rest of this is like a dream."

"Except this is my life. I can't imagine yours." She reached for the cup of iced tea and took a sip. "It must take a lot of fortitude and mental toughness to do your job."

"You make it sound noble. I don't know about that. Being a soldier is tough, sure, and there are a lot of things harder in life."

"Yes, but being a soldier has to be one of the most stressful things ever." She wasn't going to let him get away with being humble. "Under pressure, in danger, sacrificing comforts and pushing yourself so hard. It makes my life look simple."

"Everything comes at a cost, whether it's good or bad." He looked remote again, as if he had come close to telling her the truth about himself, as if he had come close to opening up and changed his mind. "What about you? You're working hard to put yourself through school. You have a goal. You could be out doing something easier with your life, but instead here you are. Forgoing comfort and fun for something more important."

"That's how you see your life. As doing something more important?"

"I do." He took another bite of his sandwich, chewing away and looking quite content to do so.

So he wouldn't have to elaborate. Oh, she had him figured out. He liked to stay on the surface of things, too. It was safer to stay closed up.

She knew how that was, so she let him have his way. She changed the subject, but not her opinion of him. No, that was going up a notch every time they met. "What does Giselle have planned for you tonight?"

"Some symphony thing. I didn't ask for details."

"The music department is putting on its midsemester concert series. It's really good. Something tells me you're not the kind of guy who appreciates Bach."

"That would be safe to say."

He was entirely far too sure of himself with that grin on his way-too-handsome face, as confident as a conquering hero. But there was more to him, glimpses of authenticity she saw beneath his shields. Bits of sadness and pieces of loss. A measure of courage and a man who tried to do the right thing. Most of all, she saw loneliness. This man, who had carried her to safety and brought her home, who sacrificed his chance for an easier life, felt out of sync with his family. He had lost his friends along the way.

She ached for him. Worse, she sort of liked him. What was the point in fighting it? She took the last bite of her sandwich, hoping she wouldn't regret what she was about to do. "Maybe you and Giselle need some company. I have season tickets. We could go together to-night."

"Do you always invite yourself along like that?"

"Never." She liked that his shadows eased and he seemed brighter, clearer, as if his armor wasn't deflecting quite as much. "Maybe I would like to go with Giselle, but since you're there you'll just have to put up with me, too."

"I think I can manage it. I'm Army-tough."

"Isn't that a commercial?"

"Yes, but that doesn't mean it's not true." He certainly looked tough enough to stand for what was right and good.

Did her heart sigh, just a little? She couldn't believe it. Of course, her heart was completely unaffected. Or was she clinging firmly to denial? She took a sip of iced tea, letting its sweet coolness reassure her. No, it was merely respect she felt for her new friend and nothing more.

Chapter Four

In the second movement of the first Brandenburg Concerto, she heard a faint rustle as the man seated beside her leaned close.

"Hand me your phone." His whisper was nearly nonexistent. His hand shot out, palm up.

"Is that an order, soldier?"

"Absolutely." That single word held a note of humor. "Do it, or it's the brig for you."

"Tempting." She handed the phone over with a smile. The question remained, what was he going to do with it? She had to lean a little closer to find out, didn't she? It wasn't as if she wanted to be nearer to him. It was a matter of necessity. She had to know what he was looking up on her phone, right?

"Interesting." He began hitting buttons. Was he putting in his phone number? Looked like it. When he pressed the phone into her hand, it was warm from his touch.

Something down deep in her spirit shivered, but she denied that, too. Apparently, she was very adept at denial. Who knew? While she was at it, she decided to deny the pain beating through her ankle and the uncomfortable swelling beneath the cast.

She tucked the phone into her purse and tried to focus on the lilt of the piccolo. But what was she aware of? Pierce as he covertly tugged his cell from his pocket, flipped it open and quietly tapped at the keys.

She was *so* not surprised when her purse began to vibrate silently. It didn't take a genius to figure out who had texted her. She bent for her phone, and when she saw the screen and his message there, she could imagine the deep intonation of his words and the warmth of his humor.

"Is it me, or is this music boring?" he'd typed.

"It's U," she typed in reply.

Out of the corner of her eye she saw him grinning. Her phone quaked and there was his message on the screen. "I'd rather be yawning."

"Sure. Considering the way U ski." She well remembered her first impression of him, the blur streaking by whooping out "banzai." Hard to imagine then that she would be sitting with him listening to a symphony. She hit Send.

He grinned at her message and texted back. "I'm not the skier with the broken ankle."

"True." How could she deny that one? "It's nice that U R enduring this."

"Giselle likes this stuff. Boggling." His reply came quick, right in time with the crescendo of the music.

"She *is* a music major." Lexie glanced over at the girl sitting on Pierce's other side. Giselle was scowling at him, as if she couldn't take him anywhere, but it was a loving look more than a censuring one. That fondness said more than anything about the man beside her.

"She's showing me what I'm missing." His words flashed on her screen. "Not working."

"Classical music isn't your thing?" she asked, expecting a certain reaction as she sent it.

His muffled snort of laughter made her smile.

"Not even close. Is it yours?" he asked.

"Yes. It's a great luv of mine." It was only the truth.

"R U kidding?" He looked shocked.

"No. Half the music on my iPod is classical." Part of her was afraid that she was a geek for confessing it. Then again, maybe it was good he knew this about her right up front. It was proof they could never be more than friends. She kept typing. "U R never speaking to me again, right?"

"Wrong." His answer was swift, as if there wasn't a moment of debate. "It's not so bad. Or U."

"Neither R U." She smiled inside as she tapped at the tiny keys. Those three words stared back at her on the screen. Did she send them?

"We're free." Pierce peered over her shoulder. "The music is over."

"No, soldier. That was only the first half." Up close, she could see the shadows in his eyes, the reminder of some of the things he had revealed to her. No one looking at him would see anything less than a good, decent and strong man. Yes, she liked him. Very much.

"The first half? You mean it's not over?" Crushed, he glanced around the emptying auditorium. The light crowd of students and townies filed down the aisles and streamed out the exits in search of refreshments. The crisp scent of coffee filled the air. Pierce stood rooted in place. "There's *more?*"

"It could be worse." She deleted her message and tucked away her phone.

"How, exactly?" he quipped, but she could tell he was only kidding. "Giselle, Lexie looks pale. I'm taking her home *if* she wants to leave early."

His hand caught hers, to help her to her feet. She felt the impact of his solid palm against hers, and it was like an avalanche's sudden strike. The earth went missing from under her feet. His iron-strong hand clasped around hers was her only anchor. Before she could draw her next breath, the floor stabilized, and she was standing without remembering how she'd gotten up. Her hand was still tucked in Pierce's.

"Y-yes," she stammered. She couldn't seem to think straight. "My ankle is really protesting."

"Pierce, I can't believe you lasted *this* long. It's a good sign." Giselle steepled her hands together, shining with happiness. "See? You like it here. I'm going to have you enrolled by Monday. I'm sure of it!"

"That's a little optimistic, kid." Affection softened his features, but it did not change his shadows. Darkness seemed a part of him as he hauled the crutches from beneath their seats and held them for her.

His nearness made her dizzy. She wrapped her fingers around the hand holds and pulled the crutches beneath her arms. Transferring her weight, she moved forward. Thank goodness there was no one left in the aisle, since the incline was hard to crutch. It didn't help that Pierce was at her side, his hand resting lightly on the small of her back as if to steady her. She did not doubt that if she slipped, he would keep her from falling.

Her palms went damp, and that didn't help the

crutching situation. Her pulse fluttered like a kite in a high wind. Probably from the exertion of heaving her body weight with every step, that was all. Nothing to worry about, right?

Right.

Giselle was keeping pace with them. "Tell him, Lexie. College is great. Don't you love it?"

"I'm certainly glad I'm here." She knew where this was leading. Poor Giselle. She had to be still grieving her brother, the one killed in action. She cast a furtive glance to the man towering beside her. His jaw tensed. His armor was up. "But remember, college isn't for everyone."

"It should be. Everything is here. Math for the math people. Science, and literature and religion. You like languages, Pierce. You could major in a language and learn Latin or something."

"I could." The strain in his jaw was the only outward sign of his unhappiness. "But it would be hard to do all that between missions."

"You aren't still going to go back in. Mom and Skip don't want you to, either."

"True, but it's my decision." A muscle ticked in his neck.

More stress? She kept crutching, feeling the pain between the siblings. The family had already lost one son. Of course they feared losing another. She reached the exit and that seemed to end the conversation as the three of them waded into the crowded foyer where vendors were making a brisk business. She said good-night to Giselle, who went off in search of her friends, and let Pierce help her into her winter coat.

"The floor is wet." His hand lingered on her shoulder, as if he didn't want to let go. "Want me to carry you?"

Carry her? Her stomach dropped four inches. Nervous tingles popped like soda bubbles through her system. She knew exactly how hard and dependable his chest was. Memories of being in his arms flooded her. While she held herself as stoic as possible, she could not forget how safe she had felt, how cozy and protected.

Not that she was attracted to him. She was definitely not looking for love, but the idea of being carried by him tonight felt a little bit like tempting fate. Best to keep things as they were and let the memories of his capable arms sheltering her fade away into forgetfulness.

If that were possible.

"I'll be careful." She wasn't entirely sure if she was referring to the floor or her out-of-place feelings. Either way, she concentrated on going slow and making sure the rubber tips of her crutches were solid before each step forward. The problem with going so slowly was that Pierce stayed by her side, a steadfast protector against the bump of the crowd and any sudden fall.

"I owe you big-time." He held the heavy glass door for her, raised his face to the wind and let the rain batter him. "Ah, freedom. The truck isn't far from here. I'll drive you home."

"I'd rather walk." She glanced sideways at him as she navigated the wet concrete. "I'm not fooled. You liked the music."

"It's not my favorite, but it wasn't half-bad. Don't tell my sister that. I'm trying to discourage her at all costs." The occasional snowflake tumbled to the ground with the rain. Looked like winter had blown itself out. "She means well, but I'm trying to keep the trip a good one."

"Why? I thought a soldier like you wouldn't hesitate

to face fire head-on." Some people could have said that judgmentally or in argument, but Lexie's alto was pure gentleness. She simply wanted to understand.

It had been a long time since someone on the home front had. Maybe that's why he felt his defenses lower enough to let his feelings in. "I'm only here for a visit. I want to keep things with my family good. Before he died, Tim hadn't done that. He'd come home for a break, argued with them when they asked him to step down, and he died before he could make it right."

"And that's why your sister is giving you the full-court press?"

"Yep." He listened to the rush of the rain in the street and the tap of it pattering against his jacket. The wind blew damp and icy, but when he shivered, it wasn't because of the cold.

"How did he die?" Her question came softly, easing past every shield he'd barricaded around that memory.

He smelled blood as it inched down the side of his face—nothing serious—and felt the grit of sand in his eyes. The grenade compression echoed in his ears, making the pop-pop-pop of machine-gun fire merely background noise.

He heard their point man shout, "Incoming!" Heard Hawk quip, "So much for our covert op," and as RPG tracer fire flashed like a laser in the dark, he saw what his brain had been trying to tell him. Something was wrong. Way wrong. He cleared his throat and brought himself back to the present.

"Tim was hit by enemy fire on a rescue mission." He put the brakes on the memory and the grief. "I was supposed to have been watching his back, but he fell right in front of me."

"You feel responsible." Not a question, a statement, kindly spoken, as if she not only knew the answer, but the depth of it.

His soul still bled. "I do."

They were silent as they crossed the street, cleared of snow, puddling with rain.

"It wasn't your fault." Her faith in him rang softly but unshakable.

"It feels that way." The memory rolled forward again, like a DVD on-screen, in the middle of a scene. The sounds of war faded. The spit of bullets into the wall next to him held no threat. All he could see was Tim on the ground, still and silent. Time had jarred to a stop. His heartbeat had crashed to a halt. The only thought in his mind had been denial. Tim couldn't be down. He was fine. He would get up any second. Rock fragments needled into his cheek and neck, but he'd felt no pain. He'd felt nothing. Tim wasn't moving, didn't look like he was breathing.

"He's gone and I'm not." He felt the weight of his brother in his arms. Heard Tim's gasp of pain. Shouted out for the corpsman, knowing it was too late. His brother's last words rang in his memory. "Tell Mom and Dad. I'm not sorry. Do-on't g-grieve. For. Me."

Sadness drowned him. He cleared his throat, forcing the memories and the grief back into the vault. "You're getting around real good on those crutches."

"You, sir, are very good at changing the subject."

"I think it's important to stick with your strong suits." He gave thanks for the cooling rain, washing away the grit of the memory on his face. "I never asked what you're majoring in."

"I'm in the counseling psychology program."

Why wasn't he surprised? The gentle questions, the faithful understanding and her ability to see deep. She would make a good counselor. "You've been analyzing me?"

"Yes. I might make you a case study." She winked, crutching slowly along. She had to be hurting, but it didn't show. Her smile was relaxed and honest. "I'm teasing you. I'm only in the first year of my graduate program, and even if I knew how, I'm not counseling you. We're friends."

She'd gotten closer faster than anyone ever had. That made him uncomfortable right there. He had a lot of choices. One of which was the easiest: he could see her to her dorm, say goodbye and that would be the end of it. Or, he could pull back a little, keep things friendly, but not so close. Knowing he would be leaving in a few days for home would make that easy. There was a third option: he could step up and follow his gut. She wasn't looking for more than a friend. He couldn't be more than one.

"That we are." He agreed, friends after all. "As I hear it, you've been a good support to my sister, as well."

"It's part of my job."

"More than that. You've helped her a lot this year. I know, because she's written enough about you. My R.A. this. My R.A. that. It's taken me a bit to piece it all together, but you were the one who helped her when she was so homesick back in September."

"She wasn't the only one. I had a homesick circle. Everyone gathered in the floor lounge and we had prayer and a support session a couple times a week."

"It meant a lot to her. And after meeting you, it means a lot to me." His voice dipped sincerely, as solemn as the night.

Why did that make her heart tug? Admiration for the man filled her. The more she got to know him, the more she liked him.

"I'm grateful for the support you've given her. You seem to get her." He paused, as if wrestling with the right words. "We talked some today. That's why I was sure she was going to let this go."

"You mean her campaign to entice you to choose college over the Army?"

"That would be the one. But she won't give up." The shadows clung to him. "Neither will I."

"She's afraid of losing you." That was something she could completely understand. Since she'd caught her breath, she crutched forward into the sting of the rain. "Have you always wanted to be a soldier? What made you want to join the military?"

"My dad was Army. When I was a little kid, I didn't think there was anything greater than wearing the uniform. I still don't."

There was the surface answer, she realized. The safest answer, the easiest. "Was he a Ranger, too?"

"Yep. He was on the ground back in Desert Storm. He had it rough. He lost a leg in an attack. He was never the same."

"I'm sorry for him. That had to be devastating."

Pierce stayed silent, letting the crescendo of the rising wind speak for him.

She tried to imagine what it would be like to give so much of your life in service. Putting on hold all the wholesome pleasures of life, free time, weekends without obligation, precious time spent with family, and one's personal dreams for discipline and duty. She tried to imagine what it was like to come home with a disability, or to be the son of a dad who might feel no longer whole.

They were halfway up the path to the dorm before he broke the silence. "Thanks for not saying it."

"Saying what?"

"That could happen to me, or worse. To die in action, the way Tim did." His throat worked, the only sign of the wound he held in secret. "Every time a soldier goes on a mission or follows an order, he does so knowing the ultimate price."

They had reached the front door, where light spilled from the portico like rain. She faced him, searching for the truth he held back, for the truth she could sense. She tried to imagine his brand of courage. "So why do you do it?"

"Because someone has to."

She saw it in his very essence, in his character and in his honor. How could her first impression of him have been so wrong? He was no ordinary man. He was a rare individual who lived his principles, and in doing so went beyond what was safe.

"Believe me, I know the risk. When I signed up I thought I was going to learn to be tough and brave. To really find out who I was. Well, I did figure out the man I am. I don't run from a fight, but I don't go looking for one, either. I've seen what happens when people have no rights and freedom, and others no conscience or no compassion."

She thought of the terrible stories on the international news, where foreign correspondents spoke of genocide and violence. She thought of the threats this nation had endured. Infinite respect for this man brimmed over, leaving tears stinging in her eyes and heavy in her soul. "You stand and fight for us all."

"When I have to. You don't realize how precious our personal freedoms are. I've seen lands where people have none. The things I have seen—"

She forgot to breathe as he towered before her, all six feet plus of him. He radiated immeasurable commitment and sorrow. He bore wounds from his fighting, deeper ones that were not visible, but she saw them.

"I've seen evil and what it can do." He remained soldier straight, soldier strong. "What you have here is precious. Having the freedom to attend college, choose your course of study and vocation. It's idyllic. This is everything I work to defend. It's why I face the fire. I'm going in for another four years so my family can live safe. So everyone's family can, too."

How could she not respect this man? How could she not admire him without end or caution? She could not keep a careful distance between them. She could not stay in denial. Not anymore.

"It's why my brother died. He understood. He wanted me to carry on for him, for both of us. It's what I intend to do. Do you understand?"

"Yes." She shifted her weight on her crutches, looking down at the damp cement, so that he could not guess how much she thought of him. "My life now feels very small in comparison."

"No, that's not what I want you to feel." Lines dug into his forehead. "That's not why I said all of this."

"I know. I should be doing more. Giving more." Her life had become so focused on getting her degree. There were tests, papers, research projects and work, all with demands and deadlines. It had consumed her. "I volunteer at church, but it's not enough."

"You're wrong." He swiped the pad of his thumb

across her cheek, catching a drop of rain wet on her skin. "You do a lot in your own way. Look at how you've helped my sister and, I'm sure, every other freshman on your floor."

"It's not saving the world." She thought of all he had given. "It's so small."

"No, you're wrong. Kindness is what makes the difference in this world. I'm surprised at you, Lexie." He cradled her chin in his hand. "Don't you read your Bible?"

"Y-you know I do." She could barely get the words out. His touch kindled a strange, new tenderness within her, one she had never felt before. It baffled her. This was not how she was supposed to be feeling.

"Being kind is a great thing. It matters more than you know." He leaned closer until he was all she could see, the only thing in her field of vision. The dark night and wash of light became nothing when compared to the man towering over her, both strong and gentle.

Everything within her stilled. Her heart had inexplicably opened.

"Good night, Lexie." His grin was reassuring. "Thanks for coming with me tonight. Even more, thanks for letting me walk you home. I feel better. More clear about what I have to do."

"Tell your family what you just told me, and they will understand."

"I will." He withdrew his touch, but not the feelings of closeness. Those feelings lingered like damp on the air, wrapping around them like an invisible tie. He opened the door for her. "Be careful on the wet floor."

"That's my plan." She couldn't tell if she went slowly because of the rain or to draw out his leaving. As soon as her crutches hit the carpet inside the foyer, she pivoted, wanting one last look at him. Would she see him tomorrow? He hadn't said either way. "Good night, Pierce."

He let the door close, walking backward out of the fall of the lights. The night claimed him, and she shivered, not from the rain, but because she was no longer close to him.

Chapter Five

"**Y**ou and Lexie are sure getting along." Giselle bubbled as he held the truck door for her after the concert was over. Her other two friends, already squeezed in the middle of the bench seat, chatted to each other about some cute cello guy.

Pierce braced himself and waited for his sister to climb into the seat. He could take a lot; he wasn't going to let her high hopes affect him. He and Lexie were not only getting along, they were clicking. His fingertips buzzed with the memory of cradling her chin. The image of empathy on her face remained emblazoned in his mind. He could not forget the closeness he'd felt to her.

"Why wouldn't we get along?" he told his sister. "She's nice. I'm nice—"

"I wouldn't go *that* far," she interrupted sweetly.

"Don't forget I'm heading back to my base in another week." He shut the door before she could argue with that. The rain had stopped, leaving the feeling of damp mist in the air. The wind battered him as he ducked his head and circled around to the driver's side. The minute he opened the door, he started talking before his sister had a chance to do more than open her mouth. "I don't have time for a relationship."

"You could make time if you really wanted to."

Everything about her was dear, from her round, sweet face to her stubbornness. He couldn't look at her without remembering the fragile little baby—six pounds, ten ounces—that had come home in Mom's arms. He always saw the little toddler prancing around the kitchen underfoot, banging the flat of her hand against her toy tambourine and singing while Mom made supper. He would always see the little sister trailing after the boys in the woods, stopping to pick a wildflower and add it to the bouquet clutched in her hand.

It was doubly complicated when he couldn't bear to argue with her. They had such precious little time left.

"Let's make this the end of the discussion." He plugged the key into the ignition and turned over the engine.

"For now," she agreed with a look that said she would come back to it.

He didn't doubt it. There wasn't much traffic, the event hadn't been that well attended, but he waited for a few other cars to pull out before he backed into the lane and wound around the concert hall, following the sinuous, mostly-empty campus roads. He liked the peace of the tall trees and careful landscape. This was the way life ought to be. Protected, safe and happy. He could see why his sister liked it here so much.

The dormitory emerged into sight from behind tall trees, all four stories aglow. Lexie was up there on the top floor, probably with her ankle elevated. Was she studying? Reading? Watching TV? He didn't like that he was wondering. He didn't like the strange dull ache in his chest.

"Thanks for the ride," the two girls said almost in unison as they hopped out of the truck after Giselle.

He let the engine idle, bolstering himself for his sister's parting words. He didn't doubt she would take a shot about Lexie.

"I'll meet you tomorrow at ten sharp for Sunday service." That was all she said, but judging by the delight dancing in her eyes, she hadn't given up her fight to find a reason for him to become a civilian.

He waited while the defroster fought at the film of fog rimming the windshield, made worse by the influx of damp air. Giselle hurried along with her friends, talking and laughing. He knew their big talk was coming; his stomach hardened and the armor went up. He feared tomorrow she would sit him down and force him to talk about Tim.

Sorrow hit him like a freight train, sending him spinning. He shut out the image of Tim's flag-draped coffin and of the other coffins over the course of his service. He pushed away those feelings, watching as the windshield blurred. Rain smeared on the glass, falling in giant sloppy drops. He flipped on the wipers and caught Giselle disappearing through the doors, safely in her dorm for the night.

If you cared about someone, it hurt more when you lost them. He put the truck in gear and circled around, headlights cutting a swatch of light through the dark. He'd come close to caring about Lexie today. She'd gotten too close to the vulnerable part of him. He wasn't used to it. He didn't like it. She made him way too uncomfortable.

That gave him something to think about on the drive back to the hotel.

Thunder resounded through the sky above and echoed in the church vestibule as Lexie balanced on her crutches. Sweet strains from the choir's opening hymn rose through the open doors to the sanctuary. Hail broke out, dropping like nails on the cathedral roof above.

"We made it just in time." Amber slipped out of her coat, ignoring the drips as she reached for Lexie's crutches. "I'll hold these if you want to take off your coat."

"I owe you big-time for this." Lexie's ankle had swollen so badly, she'd almost considered missing the service. "I'm thankful you volunteered to drive me."

"I'm just glad I could help you for a change. You've done so much for me." Amber took both coats and hung them up.

The sound of hail reverberated through the sanctuary as they made their way in. The aisles brimmed with students, faculty and families from town. Lexie tried to keep focused on not making too much noise with her crutches, but her thoughts drifted back to last night and Pierce's touch.

It was *not* the sweetest moment of her life, really, she told herself. Maybe if she said that enough, she'd believe it. It was worth a try, right? She hopped into a back row, slid her crutches under the pew and straightened for the rest of the hymn. Her ankle was throbbing, but that could work for her. It would keep her mind off Pierce.

Amber opened a hymnal and leaned close, sharing it. Lexie took her side of the book and held it open. Her eyes were supposed to focus on the page and make sense of the notes and the words, but did they?

No. For some inexplicable reason her gaze strayed up the end aisle to where a brown-haired man with impressive shoulders and perfect posture stood attentively singing. A shock of tender emotion zinged through her, both surprising and unsettling because she didn't want to feel this way.

Don't look at him, Lexie, she thought, ordering her gaze to the hymnal, but it was too late. She was singing the last notes of the hymn along with everyone else and there was nowhere to look but forward.

Why was he directly in her line of sight? As the minister began to speak and the inevitable rustling filled the sanctuary, she couldn't help noticing that Pierce wore a black suit. The well-cut jacket complimented his muscular physique. Her pulse gave a little leap, remembering last night, of what he had told her and how close they had been. That closeness scared her.

"Let us pray."

She bowed her head, welcoming the peace of prayer to her confused heart.

He'd caught sight of Lexie during the service, but with his sister in tow, he had been unable to make a beeline through the crowd after her. By the time he and Giselle had made it outside it was snowing again and she was nowhere in sight.

Right now the stack of blackberry pancakes sat like a lump in his gut. The brunch had been tasty, but the topic of conversation had not been. Giselle had done what he expected, making an all-out attempt to talk him out of returning to duty, once and for all. She'd talked about losing Tim, and how much she missed him, and how thinking about Tim made it feel as if she were dying inside. She didn't want to go through another loss like that. She didn't want Pierce to come home in a coffin.

He got that. He did. But it hadn't changed his mind and now Giselle was angry with him for not seeing reason. He'd done all he could, he told her the truth from his heart. It had made no difference.

He parked in a guest spot in front of the dorm. He didn't want to break the unhappy silence that had settled between them. If he did, would it make things worse? Frustrated, he didn't know how to fix the situation. He feared that the one person he could talk to, who might understand, was someone he really ought to avoid.

"I'm too mad at you to talk to you now," Giselle informed him as she shoved open the door. She might feel mad, but she looked sad. Tears stood in her eyes, hovering, as she slid to the ground. "Have a safe flight home."

"You take care now." He stopped short of saying anything more. His chest was knotted up good and tight. He didn't trust his voice as she shut the door, ducked her head and hurried through the snowfall. The temperature had turned cold again while they had been in the restaurant.

His cell phone beeped. A text message? He dug it out, figuring Hawk was probably keeping him updated on the ski conditions, the lucky dog.

"How did it go?" Lexie had written.

He stared at her name, and the knot in his chest yanked tighter. He began typing. "Good. Considering."

"Uh oh. How's Giselle?" her message asked.

"Mad @ me." And then some, but maybe it was smarter to keep his feelings out of it right along with Giselle's disappointment. No doubt Lexie would find out about it soon, whenever his sister chose to share it with her.

At least Lexie understands, an unwanted thought reminded him. It should have comforted him, but it only made his trapped, unnamed feelings begin to ache.

"Give her time," Lexie answered.

He stared at her words on his little screen, bright in the dark, stormy day. He was a man trained to look at a situation and make the right decision. The back of his neck tingled, like it did on the job when he'd missed something vital and was about to make a mistake. His thumbs were on the keys, ready to ask if she could meet him to talk.

Is that what he really wanted? To talk with her? He set the phone on the seat, staring at her words on the screen. Lexie's advice was meant as nothing more than a friend. They both knew it. But something had changed for him. Something he wanted to push aside and ignore, but that was never smart. That was no good solution to a problem.

He had to examine the tangled knot in his chest, hurting like a set of bruised ribs. What did he really want?

To see her again. The answer came quickly and quietly, as if spooling up from his soul. He could deal with his family. He would probably go back to active duty with their disapproval, but it had happened before.

No, he had a harder time accepting what was truly eating at him. Not only did he want to see Lexie, he needed to see her. He longed to see her sweet smile and her lovely face and the peace he'd felt with her. He missed her company and companionship and the gentle way she made him smile.

A headache began to throb, and he rubbed at his forehead with the heel of his hand. You aren't looking for anything serious, buddy. That was his number-one rule. Why did it feel as if he were in real jeopardy of breaking it? He wasn't looking for disaster. And while Lexie was a friend now, he could look down the path and see how his feelings could deepen for her. That was something he couldn't risk. He could only get hurt. That was a fact.

Maybe it was time to do the right thing for them both. He grabbed up his phone and typed a return message. "I'm heading out tomorrow."

It seemed an eternity before her answering message popped onto his screen. Her words were friendly. "To Wyoming?"

"Yep." He hit Send. He could have said more, but he didn't. He glanced through the streaks on the windshield to the warm lights of the cozy dorm. Snow landed on the glass, gathering until the wipers swiped them away.

His phone beeped. He looked down at her message. "Have a safe trip."

The ache in his chest doubled. He winced, knowing what he was walking away from. "Thanks. Take care of that ankle."

He hit Send and waited before his phone beeped. "Goodbye." Her one word said it all.

She wasn't feeling this way. He would never be a contender for a girl like Lexie, if he was looking to be. The ache in his chest became a pain that took his breath away.

He pocketed his phone, put the truck in gear and headed away from the dorm. As he drove through the campus and onto the main street through town, he banished all thoughts of her. But the feeling, and the hurt, remained.

Lexie heard the knock on her partly open door and looked up from her homework. The desk, wedged in the corner by the window, gave her a good view of the snowy trees and courtyard, but she had to twist around in her chair to see who had dropped by. "Come in."

The door swung open wider, revealing Giselle in a pair of navy blue MCU sweats. Tears stood in her eyes. "Do you have a minute?"

"For you, I have more than a minute." She closed her book and saved her computer file. "I thought you might drop by. I hear your brother is leaving for Wyoming."

Giselle nodded, lingering in the doorway. She must have been trying to study, too, because her dark hair was tied back, out of the way.

Lexie gathered up her crutches. "If you want something to drink, I've got soda in the fridge."

"No, thanks." The girl bit her lip, as if she were thinking hard, or as if what she had to say was difficult.

"Come sit down." She eased into her overstuffed reading chair and leaned her crutches against the bookcase. The pipes clanked as the radiator came to life, spewing out warm air. Lexie waited as the girl closed the door.

You're not thinking about Pierce, she reminded herself. She had to be disciplined about this. At least, until she was clear about why she was feeling this way.

"I was hoping to ask you for a favor. A really big one." Giselle slumped onto the couch. "It's about my brother."

"What about Pierce?" Her thoughts shot to his text messages and their conversation in the rain. All it took was a single thought and a spear of panic burrowed into her heart. She had gotten too close to him. If that wasn't impending doom, then she didn't know what was.

"He's going to go back in for another four years," Giselle explained, her worry for her brother evident in her voice, on her face, in her posture. "I don't want anything to happen to him. He can't see it. He thinks he's invincible or something."

"I'm sure he knows the cost of his sacrifice." She remembered the stalwart man standing as if alone in the rain. "You never told me about Tim."

"I can't stand to." Giselle bowed her head, the picture of pure grief.

"A brother's life is a lot to give for this country." She saw again the raw sadness that had etched into Pierce's face. She ached for him, too. "It's understandable you don't want to give another."

"I'm just so mad at him. He's macho, that's what this is. And headstrong. He just wants his way." Giselle sounded angry, but as she reached for a tissue from the box on the end table, her tears meant something else.

"You don't believe those things about your brother for a second." She thought of the responsibility and discipline it took to do his job, and of the irresistible gentleness he'd shown her—an impressive combination. Her chin tingled with the memory of his touch. "Pierce is a rare, truly trustworthy man."

"He is." Giselle sniffled into the tissue, fighting her tears. "I think he should go to college, get his degree and get a nice, safe job. What's wrong with that? Lots of people do it every day."

"True." Lexie remembered what he had said about his commitment to duty. Something stronger than admiration sparked to life within her. Something she simply could not let herself look at. "He's made his choice. He's not the one conflicted over this. You are, Giselle."

"I th-thought you would help me. You don't understand." Her words vibrated with heartbreak.

"You can't save him, Giselle. Only God can do that." She couldn't explain why she was hurting, too. Why Giselle's fears felt real to her, too. Maybe because she already cared too much for the man. "I'm going to help you, Giselle. Okay?"

"Okay." She sniffled harder.

Lexie handed her another tissue. "You've kept Tim's grief bottled up for too long."

"But I don't want to talk about him. I just c-can't." Giselle hung her head, so lost.

At least they had gotten to the heart of the problem. Lexie reached for Giselle's hand, offering sisterly comfort. Later she would call the student counseling center hotline for the particulars on their weekly grief support group. For now, she would offer what friendship she could, sitting with Giselle while she cried.

It had been a bad night, and the morning wasn't going much better. Pierce tossed his rucksack on the floor of the truck. His morning flight to Wyoming was delayed, and he'd gotten only a few winks of sleep. Last night's precipitation had iced dangerously to every surface and the rental truck didn't come with an ice scraper. Not that any of this qualified as a hardship in his opinion, but he was on vacation and his heart was troubled over Tim, over his family and over Lexie.

He knocked the snow off his boots and hopped behind the wheel. The defroster blazed heat, and only the most stubborn ice remained. He had some time to kill before he had to be at the airport. Hawk was already headed off to their air base, and there wasn't enough time to drive up to the ski resort.

He buckled in, debating what to do. Scratch that. He was debating over finding a way of avoiding what he ought to do. Lexie had been on his mind, the way she'd drawn him in, the way she smiled, the way he lit up when he was with her. He'd panicked yesterday. That was the plain truth. He wasn't proud of it. A bad feeling had wedged into his gut. He didn't like leaving things this way. He wanted a proper goodbye.

He put the truck in gear. The tires spun, caught, and he backed out of the parking spot. It wasn't as if he was going to fall head over heels for her, he thought as he straightened the wheel. He had learned his lesson about falling for a civilian. So, did that mean he went straight to the airport and waited around for hours? Or did he make that detour?

He didn't know what made him decide to nose the truck down the main road through town toward the university instead of away from it. It wasn't rational. He was simply following his gut. It didn't feel right to say goodbye to her in a text message. She meant more to him than that.

By the time he'd paid for parking and found a spot, the campus was quiet. Classes were in session, which meant Lexie was probably in one of those brick buildings, copiously taking notes. As he strolled along the main pathway to the quad, he could picture her at a desk, head bent over her keyboard, typing away with her fingers in a blur and her black hair falling over one shoulder.

He took shelter in the annex off the library, where a candy stand sold newspapers and hot drinks. After commandeering a bench, he punched in a text message. "Where R U?"

For all he knew, she had back-to-back classes all morning long, but he had to try. He hit Send. A pair of girls that reminded him of his sister emerged from the library and were debating over candy choices at the stand.

Giselle was wrong. He wasn't meant to be here. He tried to picture putting on this life. It looked pleasant with a backpack slung over one shoulder, grabbing a hot cup of tea between classes, chatting on the way with a few buddies. Maybe grabbing lunch at the cafeteria a few doors down, talking about books and professors.

He couldn't see it. It didn't fit. Since he was a little boy, the black and gold Ranger tab had been his dream. He had always wanted to be a Ranger. For better or worse, it was who he was. Tim had understood that. It was why he carried on, for himself and for his brother's memory. It was his calling.

God, he prayed, *if You want me on another path, then I will be waiting with eyes peeled for You to show me the way. Otherwise, I will remain committed.*

His cell beeped. He thumbed the read button, pulse kicking.

"I'm @ the libe. Where R U?" she'd written.

"Outside the libe. Want lunch?" he sent, half

worried that she would turn him down. He popped off the bench and took a stroll. It wasn't nerves or anything, well, maybe a little. He was surprised how much he wanted to see her. Why wasn't she texting back? Had he made a mistake?

Chapter Six

"Pierce?"

Her gentle voice surprised him. He looked up, happiness lighting him at the sight of her. Her hair was down, spilling over her shoulders like liquid ebony. She wore a blue ski cap and her winter coat, crutching in careful steps across the wet brickwork. He raced to meet her. "It's got to be divine intervention. You don't have a class?"

"Not until after lunch." She paused to let him take her backpack. "Thanks. Seeing you was the last thing I expected. Aren't you supposed to be on a plane?"

"They put me on a later flight. I have some serious time on my hands." He slung her backpack over his shoulder. It was heavy, and kept by her side as they ambled down the breezeway. "I had nothing to do and the only other person I know in town, whom I'm not related to, is you."

"I'm glad I won out by default. I'm not complaining." She let him open the heavy glass door for her. Tables, mostly empty, were pleasantly spaced around the roomy dining area. They faced the ceiling-to-floor windows looking out at the crisply white campus grounds. "I'm happy to help you waste some time."

"Excellent." He nodded toward the tables. She was fully aware of a number of women's heads turning as she led the way through the room and grabbed a table. Oh, it wasn't her that was garnering all the attention, but the six-foot-one hunk at her side.

"This place smells good." He pulled out a chair for her and helped her scoot it in. "Is that pizza?"

"You have a discerning nose."

"One of my many talents." His dimples flashed as he leaned her crutches against the window. "What's your pleasure?"

"Their pepperoni and sausage is divine." She pulled out the chair beside her, for him to place her backpack on. "Get plenty of cheesy sticks."

"As you wish." He winked. "Anything else?"

"A cola would be good."

"It's a risky mission, but a worthy one. I'll be back ASAP." He left her smiling, striding toward the turnstiles, and disappeared into the food court.

Was that a sigh? She unzipped her coat, annoyed at herself. So, the guy was dazzling. He wasn't going to affect her. It was simple behavioral theory. Every time she felt a glitter of affection, she would associate it with something negative—how she felt when Kevin showed his true colors. That ought to work.

"Lexie." Cari Paulson slipped into a chair across from her. "Who's the hunk?"

"Giselle Granger's older brother." She was in research methods and stat with Cari. "Have you started your paper yet?"

"No. Is he your boyfriend?"

"What gave you that idea?" If she leaned a little to the right, she could see him standing at the pizza place. He radiated vitality, dressed in a jacket, sweatshirt and jeans. There was something amazing about him. Something that no other guy in the place possessed.

Wait a minute. There she was, admiring him again. Time to remind herself of what happened when she trusted a man. Disaster. Abandonment. Heartbreak.

"If that guy was taking me to lunch and he wasn't my boyfriend, he would be by the time lunch was over." Cari hopped out of the chair. "Just a little advice. See you in class."

"Yeah." She blinked. She was hardly aware of Cari crossing over to the far side of the dining room where two other students sat at a table heavy with opened textbooks. She could no longer see Pierce. He had stepped out of her sight, leaving an odd sense of loss. Cari's words sent a shiver of panic through her.

I have a crush on him, she realized, as she slipped out of her coat and hung it over the back of the empty chair. Pierce was striding toward her carrying two trays. The sight of him filled her like a smile. He walked with unmistakable confidence—she liked that about him. She liked everything she knew about him.

"Lots of cheesy sticks, as ordered." He slid the trays on the table. "You've got it made here. Everything from cinnamon rolls to deluxe pizza, and it's all good."

"Surely you get that in the Army."

"Not that the Army cooks don't try, but I've eaten out of cans for months at a time." He eased into the chair across from her. "We've talked a lot about me lately. It's your turn."

"Uh-oh. I don't think a guy like you would be interested in me." She took a straw from the tray and tore off the paper. It gave her something to do so she wouldn't have to see the truth on his face. She was going to bore the poor man.

"Why would you say that?"

"You slide down those ropes out of helicopters and go on nighttime missions, don't you?" She knew enough about guys to know they liked the pursuit, but once they reached their destinations, many of them moved on. Or, she thought as she poked her straw into the fizzing cola, maybe she simply didn't want to let him that close to her.

"Don't think that because I didn't choose to go to college I don't value it." He ripped the paper off his straw and torpedoed it into his soda. His smile was pure trouble. "Why psychology?"

"They say you gravitate toward what you need most, which in my case is maybe therapy." She was more of a complicated mess than she'd realized, because his smile made her spirit brighten like the east at dawn.

"Therapy? You think you're dysfunctional? No way."

"You don't know me well enough to make that call, believe me." It was easier to make light of things and to keep him from getting too close again. "I have abandonment issues. I have trust issues. All that leads to commitment issues. I don't want to let anyone too close."

"Me, too." He balled up the straw wrapper and flicked it onto his tray. "That's not dysfunctional, not in my opinion. It's being smart. People can let you down. That's why I like being a Ranger. The guys I work with, we depend on each other. I know the man beside me won't let me down, just like I'm going to be there for him."

"I see that about you." Yep, she definitely was suffering from a minor crush on the guy. "I understand problems, since I have so many."

"Who doesn't?"

"Exactly." She did her best not to look up at him. If she didn't look into his sensitive hazel eyes, then maybe she could keep this crush thing under wraps. "Do you want to say grace this time?"

"The pizza fumes are getting to you?"

"Something like that." It was him, purely him. She folded her hands and bowed her head.

"Father," he began in his rumbling baritone. "Thank You for this borrowed time with a new friend. I have a feeling that down the line we will both be grateful for it."

Her heart turned over, filling with gratitude. She was grateful, too. She did not trust love, but she trusted Pierce. She trusted his friendship for now and maybe for a long time to come. Maybe that's all this crush was—simple respect for a new friend. It was a comforting thought. "Amen."

"Now, let's dig into the pizza." He grabbed for a piece with everything on it. "Something tells me you're a knife-and-fork kind of pizza eater."

"There is nothing wrong with that." She took her fork in hand, surprised how good it felt to laugh with him.

"After all night marching down the mountain, I was done. Hawk, he's the stoic one, he could have been dying and you never would have known it." Pierce washed down his last bite of pizza with the last of his cola. Since Lexie still seemed interested, he kept going with the story. "Keep in mind we had our rucks on—forty pounds on our backs. We'd been hustling as fast as we could go since dark. We'd been under mock ambush three times. No chow, no breaks, nothing. Two hours' sleep the night before. I was toast. Every muscle I had was screaming fire. I came off that mountain and saw a line of pink on the horizon."

"Dawn?" She sipped on her straw daintily, the way she did everything. "You must have wanted to shout with joy."

"Sure, but I didn't have the energy. I just wanted to collapse." He still remembered that march in Ranger School. Every time life got hard or the battle got tough, he remembered how hard he'd pushed himself and it gave him confidence to keep going.

"I can't imagine that much marching. Mostly because I'm not very athletic." She put down her cup, smiling prettily. "I could probably make it a mile if I had to and then I'd collapse. I'm a wimp."

"No, you're just not conditioned. You're no wimp. You broke your ankle and didn't shed a single tear."

"I'm sure it was because the cold helped. I was too numb to actually feel it." She dipped her chin, as if embarrassed, or not used to compliments.

His chest tugged with emotion. He liked her. There was no sense fighting it. "I was in charge, and I didn't know what I was doing, but I thought I'd got us to our next post. Next thing I hear is our instructor shouting out, 'Heavy drop will be here in five minutes.' Guess what fell out of the sky?"

"I'm afraid to ask."

"A tank. It hit the ground like an earthquake. It was the next part of our mission. We trained until midnight, nonstop, but I made it. Hawk made it." He crumpled up his napkin and dropped it onto his tray. "When Tim went through the next year, he was the top of his class. Best at everything. He had all of our best advice, so I figured Hawk and I made the difference, it wasn't him."

"You never let him live it down."

"Not when he started reminding us of his accomplishments." The hardest part was remembering. The only thing worse was not remembering at all. He reached for Lexie's plates and began stacking them on top of his. "Guess it's about that time. You've got class and I've got a bird to catch."

"Is it going to be hard to go home?" Her question was kind and layered with meaning. She wasn't asking about the conflict with his folks. She was asking about Tim.

"It'll be my first visit home since his funeral." He moved her tray beneath his and tried not to feel anything. "I got leave. I escorted him home. I was a pallbearer. I stayed a couple days. My mom was inconsolable. My stepdad couldn't look at me. So yeah, I think it might be a rocky visit."

"You can call me anytime. I'm a good listener."

"I'd like that." He would miss her when he was gone. There was no sense in analyzing that too much. He wanted to keep things simple. He had another four years ahead of him with no-notice deployments, constant missions and endless training. An arduous road and sometimes a deeply lonely one. He put on his coat. "How are your letter-writing skills?"

"Top-notch. I might not be able to do a Long Range

Reconnaissance Patrol, but I am a faithful letter writer." She stood to reach for her crutches.

He beat her to it. "I'm going to put you to the test on that."

"The real question, soldier, is how good of a letter writer are you?"

"Fair to middling. It's not a skill we tackled in Ranger School." He held her crutches while she shifted onto them and grabbed her backpack from the chair. "My failing could be one reason Cindy lost interest in me."

"If she had really loved you, she would have stayed interested." Lexie seemed sure of it.

"Few relationships can take the strain. I'm just being practical." He grabbed the trays and spotted the receptacle near the door. He had become a very practical man. "In a year from now, you'll get an e-mail from me and think, Pierce, now what does he look like again?"

"No, *that's* what you will be thinking about me." She kept her head down, and her dark hair fell forward to hide most of her face, but not enough.

He saw the vulnerability there. The fear that even something as safe as a friendship would wind up hurting her in the end.

He was afraid of that, too. Just like he was scared of the deeply felt need to lay his hand against her cheek and lift her face to his. He ached for the closeness they had shared and for her gentle caring. More than that, he wanted to hold her close, to feel her sweet presence against his chest and to know the tenderness of her kiss.

Not going to happen. But still, he wanted it. He tucked it into a wish, like so many other things he could not have. A man made choices and lived with the consequences. It was smart to remember how much love could hurt and to stay away from it. Friendship was best. It wouldn't hurt so much when it was over.

"C'mon, I'll walk you to class." He held the door for her. It was starting to get busy with students pouring out of buildings and streaming down the breezeway. He protected her from the jostle as they crept into the traffic flow. He stuck by her as they followed the pathway toward a cluster of stately brick buildings. "What do you have next?"

"Research methods and statistics." Snowflakes fell between them, clinging to her hair, gracing her with sweetness. "Sounds like a blast, right?"

"Like serious excitement." He joked. "Statistics is way over my head. Does that mean you have a research project, like an experiment?"

"I'm supposed to start one. It's going to be part of my master's thesis." She paused to get a better grip on her handles and kept going. "The big problem is me. I don't know what I want to research. I keep praying for inspiration, but so far, nada."

"It will come to you when you least expect it. I have every confidence in you." They were approaching the shadow of the building, where fine flecks of snow fell between them like a veil. "Write and tell me how it works out."

"If you text me your e-mail addy."

"Deal." He held the door for her, stepping to the side to allow a few other fast-moving students by. "I hope your ankle heals up quick."

"I'll let you know when I'm back to running around without my sticks." She knew what he was doing, because she did it, too. Drawing out their final parting. It was funny how fast you could bond with one person, and how you could know a thousand others for twice as long and not like as much. "I'll keep you in my prayers, Pierce. For a good visit home."

There was more, but she couldn't say it. Her feelings were too sentimental and vulnerable, and he might take them the wrong way. She well understood Giselle's concerns. It was tough to know in a short while he would be heading back to danger, facing gunfire or worse. "Take care of yourself."

"Sure, as long as you do the same." He flashed his dimples, showing her his easy smile and charm. The serious man she'd come to know had vanished. Once again he looked very much like the guy shouting "banzai" as he barreled down the mountainside, all carefree confidence. "I'll be looking for that e-mail."

"Goodbye, Pierce." She forced her crutches forward, over the slick threshold and onto the industrial carpet running through the marbled foyer. She caught sight of his wave, of the smile sliding away. He gave her one solemn look before he turned, striding through the snowfall. She memorized the straight span of his shoulders, the powerful line of his back and the way snow veiled him like a dream.

Sure, they might keep in touch by e-mail for a while, but this could well be the last sight she ever had of him. Four years was a long time, and chances were their paths would never cross again. Sad, she tightened her grip on her handles and headed down the hallway to her next class.

The electronic doors swished apart, giving him a face full of fresh, Wyoming air. He breathed deep, scenting the mountain air and wood smoke and something innately comforting. There was no place like it on earth. It was home.

The airport was small with minor commotion. A couple of vehicles sat along the curb with family members waiting, their rapid conversations rising and falling with the cadence of the wind.

He didn't spot his folks' rig anywhere. Mom and Skip must be running a few minutes late. His plane had landed eight minutes ahead of schedule, of all things. He parked on a bench and kept watch for them. And if he pulled out his cell, it wasn't because Lexie was on his mind. She hadn't been; he'd made sure of that. He had banished her from his thoughts the moment he'd driven away from campus. Whatever his feelings for her, they had best stay buried. He'd done the right thing, said goodbye, and got the chance to see her one last time. Chances were she'd forget him by month's end.

He turned on his cell, in case Mom was trying to get a hold of him and not because he hoped Lexie might have sent a text. Because if he let himself hope, he would be bound for disappointment. Lexie was great—but he simply wasn't the man for her. An electronic beep told him he had a message waiting.

"Pierce!" Mom waved at him from their moving vehicle.

He was on his feet, emotions raw. She looked good. Older, but good. He took in her shock of gray hair, which hadn't been there last summer, and more lines on her face. Grief had been tough on her, but her smile was the same. He put thoughts of Lexie on hold as the rig's door opened and Mom rushed into his arms.

"You are a sight for sore eyes, dear boy," she told

him, grabbing hold of his jaw to take better stock of him. "You look tired and too thin. We'll fix that real fast."

"Don't tell me you've been baking up a storm just for me."

"Skip likes my baking, too, so I'm sure he and Sean can help out. Now get in this vehicle so we can get home. I can't wait to show you the new horses." She clung to him a little too long, and it was revealing.

He winced, wishing he could be what his mother wanted, but in doing that, he would let Tim down. He couldn't win. Torn up, he stowed his ruck and hopped into the backseat.

"Good to see you, Pierce," Skip said, catching his eye in the rearview mirror. "You buckled up?"

"I am now." He reached for the strap as the SUV rolled away from the curb. It wasn't until he went to secure the buckle that he realized his cell was clutched in his left hand. He flipped it open, only half listening to his mother's plan for the rest of the afternoon. His heart was pounding as if he'd just finished running ten clicks.

"Here's my e-mail addy," Lexie had written. "Tag, you're it."

He smiled; he couldn't help it. She hadn't waited for his text. She had sent her address instead. Why that made him happy, he couldn't rightly say.

"Pierce, are you listening to me?" Mom asked.

"I am now." He slipped his phone in his pocket, gladness filling places that had long been sad.

Chapter Seven

The crutches made life interesting, but she was adapting. She leaned her sticks against her bedroom wall, balancing on her good foot, and unslung the duffel bag from around her neck and shoulder. Sure, she could have asked one of the freshmen for help, but it was the crunch time before midterms. Besides, she was doing all right on her own.

She upended the bag and fresh laundry tumbled onto her twin bed. Warm from the dryer, her socks and sweats crackled, scenting the air. A knock on the door interrupted any stray thoughts of actually folding the clothes.

"It's me." Giselle lingered in the doorway. She looked pale, her eyes too big for her face. "I wanted to thank you for hooking me up with the support group."

Lexie shut the inner door to her bedroom. "I was about to head down and knock on your door to see how it went. It was good?"

"Really helpful." She sighed, looking downcast, but better somehow. "There was another girl who had lost a sister over there."

"You're not alone." Lexie leaned on her crutches. "That's a lot to handle on your own. You don't need to bottle things up. You can come talk to me anytime, you know. The center has some good counselors."

"I have an appointment on Monday." Giselle shrugged. "I think it will help."

"Good. I think it will, too."

"I'm going home this weekend. Pierce is paying for my ticket." The girl blinked hard, as if she were fighting tears and more. "We're going to get the whole family together and have an old-fashioned hog roast at Uncle Frank's. That way Pierce will have a good send-off."

She hadn't heard from him, but he was probably busy and it had only been two days. Guys never hurried about getting back to you, whether it was romantic or not. "You sound more accepting of his choice."

"Just resigned, I guess. I want to support him, but I'm really scared for him." Tears welled up and she blinked them back.

"I would be, too." She tried not to think of her feelings for Pierce. "We just want him to be safe."

"Yeah. I'm going to keep hoping he'll change his mind, but I know he won't. He's always been stubborn."

"I think he's trying to do what's right." And if she didn't like the idea of Pierce being in danger, she also had to admit that she'd never met anyone so innately capable. Giselle stayed for a few more minutes, talking of less painful things before she excused herself to go study. She, too, had a mound of work waiting her.

At least things were going better for the girl. Lexie hunkered down at her desk, eyeing her stack of research books and the third draft of her research paper sitting in the printer, awaiting final tweaking and a good proofread. This was the reason she'd met Pierce, she thought, lifting the fifteen pages from the printer tray. She had put off researching the project so she could go skiing. Remembering him was like sipping chamomile tea; it warmed her in a cozy, nice way.

So she was thinking of him with a smile on her face as she woke up her laptop and saw the message. She had three new e-mails in her in-box. Her pulse fluttered with a tiny smidgeon of hope. Not that she was waiting for an e-mail from him, she reminded herself. It was best to ward off disappointment. Pierce didn't have time to e-mail her. So exactly why was she forgoing her work to double-click on her mail program?

Her eyes zeroed in on the screen. His name was at the top of the list. She opened it, breathless, wondering what he had to say. Were things going well with his family? Or did he need a supportive shoulder?

Hey Lexie,

I've got a spare minute, so I'm borrowing my brother's laptop. Sean doesn't know it's missing yet. It'll be interesting to see if I can finish this e-mail before he figures it out. My mom has been stuffing me with all my favorites—chocolate cake with cream cheese frosting, homemade pot roast and gravy, breakfast with all the trimmings. I think she's spoiling me to make it impossible to leave. I've never had it quite this good.

She reached for the cup of tea that had been cooling on her desk and took a soothing sip. More like Mrs. Granger was so glad to have her son home safe and sound, she was spoiling him. She could picture the kind family gathering around their son. She kept reading.

Skip, my stepdad, took us up into the back country for some late season snowmobiling yesterday. This afternoon, cross-country skiing is on the agenda. Earlier in the morning, my mom dragged me to her church group meeting. The Ladies' Aid stuffed me with cookies and pinched my cheeks. Lots of the ladies remembered when I was knee-high to a grasshopper. It's weird being back home. It's like beaming down into a time warp. The ranch is the same, with horses and cattle grazing and fence always needing repairing. Skip doesn't want me to help him with the work while I'm here. I'm frustrated. So tomorrow morning after my run, I'm going to commandeer the ranch truck and head out to fix the east fence line. By the time he figures out what I'm up to, it'll be too late to stop me.

What's your day like? How's the ankle? Write when you can and save me from my family. I need contact with someone normal. Help!

Best,

Pierce.

A knock at her door broke into her thoughts. "Lexie?"

"Hi Amber." She hated turning away from her computer screen, but she was glad to see another of her favorite girls. Okay, all the girls on her floor were her favorite. "What can I do for you?"

"I was hoping I could ask your opinion on something?" Amber leaned against the door frame, one hand behind her back. "It's for my intro to American lit class. I have my paper done early, but now that I've had all this time to think about it, it's probably awful. Would you look at it?"

"I'd be happy to. I don't know how useful my opinion will be, but I'll do my best."

"Thanks." She smiled and slipped the paper on the small coffee table. "No rush. It's not due until Friday."

"I'll read it next," she promised as the girl flashed a relieved smile and took off down the hall.

She turned back to her computer.

Dear Pierce,

Here I am, writing to your rescue. (Sorry about the awful pun!) Although I'm sure your family is great. Don't forget that I know your sister, who is one of the nicest girls on my floor. Have you talked to her lately? You might want to give her a call. :)

Sure, go ahead and torture me with visions of snowmobiling and life on the ranch. My uncle's place is a cattle ranch, and I work for his family every summer. Talk about the best summer job. I get to take care of calves, ride horses and swim in the creek when it's too hot. Which sounds really good right now, because another cold front has decided to dump a new foot of snow on us. Since crutches and snow don't mix well, I'm limiting my sojourns to class, chapel and work, which gives me lots of extra time in my room to catch up on my homework. Yippee. (That wasn't a sarcastic yippee—well, not *too* sarcastic!)

The ankle is good. Sore, but the swelling is going down. I've spent my afternoon going up and down the elevator with my laundry and finishing the last draft of a research paper that's due tomorrow. I start my shift at the library at six, so it's an early dinner and then sitting at the reference desk until ten. A thrilling day—not! But remember, you asked. That will teach you.

Are your folks giving you a hard time? Or accepting your decision?

Write when you can (or when you can borrow your brother's computer again),

Lexie.

She ran a quick spell check and sent it, wondering what he was up to this afternoon. There were so many details she didn't know about his day. Was it snowing where he was, too? Was he out skiing? Hollering "banzai" as he blazed a trail through the snowy meadows?

"Lexie?" Rose was at the door. "You wouldn't have a paper clip, would you?"

"Just a sec." She pulled open her top desk drawer in search of the cylinder of colorful paper clips. She spotted it and offered it to the girl. "Here you go."

Another successful mission. Rose chose a yellow coated paper clip with thanks and bopped out of the room.

Look at the full life she had. She should be focusing on reading Amber's paper, on finishing her own paper and on the rest of a very busy day. So there was no explanation why she was missing Pierce, or why she was looking forward to his next e-mail.

She listened while she worked, but there was no telltale beep to signal that a new message was in her in-box.

"Pierce!" Mom's voice echoed in the upstairs hallway.

"I'm not here," he bellowed back as he finished

reading Lexie's letter. He poked his head down the hall and sneaked a look over the banister. No sign of his brother pounding his way through the house.

Their old sheepdog, Roger, lifted his head from his bed next to the couch and gave him a long look.

"Keep watch for me, will you, boy?"

The dog blinked, as if he understood perfectly. With Roger on the job, Pierce sat back down and started to type.

Lexie,

Glad to hear you're getting around all right. You were fairly impressive on those crutches. I hope they don't have you stuck on the reference desk until your ankle heals. That's a long time, and anything with the word *reference* in it, can't be exciting.

We only have ten acres here, enough for a few beef cows and a dozen horses. Your uncle's ranch sounds like Uncle Frank's spread. Big and wonderful and full of things to do. Whenever Mom got tired of dealing with the four of us all day long (no school), she would ship us over to Uncle Frank's to stay. We would run wild with our cousins, play in the river all day, camp out in the woods for nights on end. I can see you rolling your eyes. I know what you're thinking. *That's* why he's the way he is.

What can I say? It's true.

Hope your paper, your work and your life are going great.

Best,

Pierce.

He hit Send, his senses went on alert. Downstairs, Roger gave a low "woof." Too late. Footsteps whispered on the carpet. Was Sean coming? He moved out of his chair stealthily and edged up to the door. The muffled hush of footsteps rustled closer. He waited for the precise moment and shot out the door, wrapping an arm around Sean's neck. They tumbled to the floor with a crash.

"You're getting slow, big brother." Sean laughed, wrestling for the advantage.

"You're the slow one." He countered, keeping Sean square on the shag carpet. "I'm not the lazy one without a job. Hello."

"I'm a misunderstood genius." The old family joke. Pierce rolled his eyes.

Roger woofed in warning, sharper this time. Trouble was on the way.

"Mom's coming!" They said in unison, falling apart. Although they were grown, neither of them wanted to get in the doghouse with her. He stood up, straightening his wrinkled shirt.

"What are you boys doing up there?" She stood midway up the staircase, giving them a firm look. It was at odds with her soft curls, dimpled chin and ruffled apron.

"He took my computer, Mom." Sean might be twenty-four, but he sounded twelve.

"I was going to bring it back," Pierce found himself arguing just like old times.

"Did you hear that, Mom? Are you going to ground him or something?"

Pierce smiled at their mom, knowing her firm look held no substance. She wasn't mad at either of them. She was a complete softy.

"Pierce, you give that computer back. And boys, no more fighting in the house." She gave them one long-lasting scowl of warning before heading back downstairs.

"What were you doing with it anyway?" Sean asked. "You're not exactly a computer geek. Were you writing to your girlfriend?"

"As if a girl would have me." The best defense was a great offense. He doubted anyone in his family, Giselle included, would understand his friendship with Lexie. "Just like no girl will have you, Sean."

"Hey, I'm in a dating dry spell right now." He launched out; Pierce ducked and countered and took him down. They hit the ground, a loud thump echoed down the hall, and Roger barked enthusiastically. Mom came marching their way.

"Enough, you two, or no dessert for either one of you." She sounded fierce, but her eyes were laughing. If he looked hard enough, he could see she was biting down on her lip to keep from howling. "Honestly, I don't know what it is about you boys. It's a wonder I have a house left. Now straighten up, both of you."

"Yes, ma'am." He unhooked his arm from around Sean's neck. It was amazing what he had to put up with just to borrow a computer. The only thing missing was Tim, who would have thrown himself into the fight and caused even more havoc.

That was the cost of war, a lost soldier's life. Pierce knew wherever Tim was in heaven, he was missing them, too.

Lexie drowned out the hustle and bustle of the dining hall and ignored the loud drone of conversations. Friday evenings were especially loud, since everyone was in good spirits. Instead of grabbing a table with friends or with some of the girls from her floor, she'd taken over a small table near the window. Her laptop fit nicely next to her tray of turkey noodle casserole and a big plate of green salad.

She took a swig of iced tea, wondering what to say in her next e-mail. Pierce was probably dining with his family right now, reunited after long months apart. It sounded as if he had a good family life, in spite of his parents' divorce. They had that in common, too.

There were a lot of surprising similarities between them. They had both given up on love. They were both Christians. They had grown up in Wyoming, although in different parts of the state. It felt as if she had known him a long time, although it hadn't been long at all, which would be scary if not for the fact he would be returning to his Army life and she wouldn't really have to take a close look at her fears of commitment and intimacy.

Still, a lingering unsettled feeling remained. She closed her computer and tucked it into her backpack. She *could* put off answering him. Maybe it was caution, or maybe it was fear. Either way, she was spending way too much time thinking about him.

An electronic ring interrupted her. Her cell phone. She dug it out of her pocket. "Hello?"

"Guess who."

She recognized his friendly baritone. "Pierce Granger. I didn't expect to hear from you so soon."

"Sorry to disappoint you, but I had some time on my hands and couldn't think of anything better to do than to call you." His tone said otherwise.

Why she brightened from hearing that, she couldn't say. Maybe because it was good to hear his voice. Best not to analyze that too much. "Giselle made it home safe and sound, I assume."

"Yep. She's with Mom doing the dishes, deep in girl talk. Like I told you, it's strange. Some things never change, even when everything has."

She could see clearly what he didn't say. "While your brother is gone, your family is still there. Life goes on, like it did before."

"That's it. It's nice. Skip and Sean are out feeding the horses. I was going to borrow Sean's computer to try to instant message you, but this time he really hid it good. I'll find it, but it's going to take a little more effort."

"I have every faith in you."

"Good, because failure isn't an option."

She could picture his big smile, the one that reached all the way to his eyes and made dimples bracket his lean mouth. Total charm, made all the more awesome for the substance beneath.

"I owe you a big thanks." His voice grew serious and low. "Giselle told me about the support group."

"I only made one call and held her hand. No thanks necessary." She was glad she was able to help. She was doubly glad to hear his relief. "Have they talked you out of the Army yet?"

"No chance of that. How come you can understand when they can't?"

"I don't have the same expectations as your family does." She took a sip of her tea, surprised to find she was still seated in the crowded dining hall. "It has to be hard to be torn between what your family wants for you and what you have to be."

"That's one tough journey, walking your own path. God doesn't always mark the way well, but you've got to keep faith and keep on trekking." He cleared his throat. Maybe he'd had enough serious talk. "Tomorrow we're going over to Uncle Frank's ranch for the day. He's firing up the barbecue pit and having all the family over."

"I've never been to a hog roast, although my aunt and uncle smoke ham for family get-togethers. It sounds like fun."

"It usually is. Every woman in the family bakes up her best dishes. It's the best potluck ever."

"My mom's side of the family does that, too. It's funny how we grew up so alike."

"You ran wild in your youth, too?"

"Ha! That's an image." She could see him as a little boy, brown hair wind-ruffled as he raced through mountain meadows. "I was a quiet child. If I was outside, I was under a tree in the shade with my nose in a book."

"I was a Hardy boy fan, myself. I read every one of them. In the summers, Mom would pack us a lunch and we would take off for our tree fort. We would spend most of the day on top of that platform, keeping lookout for enemies and digging into our books. We'd spend day after day that way."

"I can picture that. Something tells me you did more than read."

"True. Sean would trail along with us most of the time, but he was the one who held down the fort when Tim and I got antsy and needed a little more adventure."

"Adventure?"

"We would take off into the hillside, climbing over downed trees and trailing through the woods. There were animals to track—deer, elk, moose, cougar and the occasional bear. It was fun following the tracks and every once in a while we ran into one of the animals. We'd sit in the brush, still as stones, just watching."

"There was a creek on our land, that my aunt and uncle own now. My cousins and I used to wade in it. When we were older, we used to go swimming where it ran deep. Fun memories."

"When we were shipped off to Uncle Frank's place we did serious damage. We put a rope in a tree so we could swing out into the river. Foolhardy. Could have killed ourselves, but what Uncle Frank didn't know didn't hurt us, I guess."

"You were one of those kids always floating the river or jumping off train trestles, weren't you?"

"Guilty. Let me guess. When you weren't a mild-mannered reader or a cautious swimmer in a sensible creek—"

"Hey, it's better to be sensible than sorry!" Was that the way he saw her? She blinked and realized that once again she was still in the cafeteria. Talking with him transported her entirely. She'd forgotten her food, which had to be seriously cool by now. When she glanced at the clock above the door, she was shocked. She had twenty minutes to go before work. Where had the hour gone? She forked in a mouthful of turkey and noodles, chewing fast.

"I wasn't knocking being sensible," he was saying. "You always have to be careful in water. I couldn't resist the urge to tease you. You are always the good one, aren't you? You always try to do the right thing."

"I try. I don't know how well I do. I feel like I always make a mess of things in the end." Like with him. She already had a serious crush on a man who couldn't be more wrong for her. A man who could never be anything more than a friend. Wasn't that a colossal mess?

Uh, yeah. She had no idea how to stop her feelings. "My cousin and I would take the horses up into the forest. That was probably my favorite thing."

"I like horses best from a distance. I prefer something more predictable, like a snowmobile or a dirt bike."

"Wait a minute, you grew up around horses, but you don't like them?" She stuck her fork in her salad, spearing a mouthful of greens. "I think there's something the big strong brave Ranger isn't telling me."

"Not all country boys grow up liking horses."

"Uh, my cousins did. C'mon, spill. You had a bad experience you never overcame."

"How did you know?"

"Happened to one of my cousins, too. He fell off his pony and he didn't get back in the saddle ever." She took a quick bite.

"I know how he feels. I used to see a horse and my knees would knock together."

"I don't exactly believe you. Aren't Rangers supposed to be tough?"

"That's a big rumor. Sad but true."

She loved how he could make her laugh. "Too bad I can't put you to the test, Mr. Tough Guy. I would invite you to ride horses with me this summer, but you'll probably be off traveling the world."

"With any luck, I won't be too far away. I'm stationed at Fort Lewis, over in Washington State. You never know. I have more leave coming, but I can be sent anywhere at a moment's notice, so I probably won't be able to show up to your challenge."

"I hear the joy in your voice."

"I'm trying to hide my relief, but it didn't work, huh?"

"Not a bit, buster." She was grinning ear to ear, and it was because of him, this man who was hundreds of miles away, but made her feel like he was in the next room. "I've got to shovel down the rest of my dinner in the next two minutes and race over to the libe. I'm working tonight."

"I don't want you to race in the snow." His tone lowered, intimately, tenderly. "I'll let you go. Goodbye, Lexie."

She couldn't make herself say goodbye, for some reason. Yes, she cared way more than was safe or sensible. "Adios."

She disconnected, although she held the phone for a moment longer than necessary as if to somehow keep the connection with him, a tie she didn't need and he didn't want.

Somehow she was going to have to deal with her feelings. Luckily, now wasn't the time.

Chapter Eight

He was beat, but it was good to be back home. He tossed his ruck on the floor, pulled his keys out of the door and hit the lights. He'd been lucky to get the little one-bedroom apartment. It was a stone's throw from the air base, but it echoed around him as he shouldered the door shut. Everything looked the same as when he'd left, sparsely furnished with secondhand stuff and covered with a layer of dust. He tossed the stack of mail on the end table along with his keys.

The flight back had been uneventful, just like the ride through traffic. Rain pattered at the windows as he grabbed the remote and punched the TV on for background noise. A basketball game buzzed as he grabbed a root beer from the fridge. His laptop sat silently blinking at the dinette table. Sure, he was toast, but maybe he could check his e-mail. It wouldn't hurt, right?

He took a cold swig of soda, but that didn't cleanse away the hope he felt. He was looking forward to Lexie's e-mail. Life had been hectic, they'd spent the weekend at Uncle Frank's, and he hadn't had a chance to borrow a computer and get online.

He pulled out the chair and vaulted into it, waiting while the laptop woke up and dialed in. His in-box was full. He had to wade through advertisements and family notes. There, nearly the last e-mail, was Lexie's. She had written him early Saturday morning. Yep, he could picture her starting her day early, hunkered down at her desk already studying.

He leaned forward, forgetting how tired he was and how long the day and forced his blurry eyes to focus.

Pierce,

It was great actually talking to you. I'm guessing that's going to be a rarity from now on. How did the hog roast turn out? How did it work out with your family?

Nothing eventful on this end. I'm sure you are rolling your eyes thinking, how did I get the most boring pen pal in the world?

What can I say? I'm studying for a quiz in my research and stat class. I've got a floor meeting this afternoon and work tonight. I think I can hear you yawning in boredom. I know, it's mundane when I write about it, but I like my life. I have the feeling you like yours, too.

Write when you can,
Lexie.

He opened a new message and started to type.

Lexie,

Don't apologize for the mundane. You could be operating under a false impression of my job. They say war is ninety percent boredom and ten percent terror. It's true from my experience. I never asked about your spring break. Isn't that coming up? I can't see you heading off to Mexico or Florida. Let me guess. You plan to put in extra shifts at the library. Am I right?

The hog roast was a blast. Uncle Frank has a gift with a barbecue pit. It was a family reunion of sorts. Got to catch up with my cousins, sit around the campfire roasting marshmallows for s'mores and shooting the breeze. Just like old times.

He stopped typing, wondering if that was enough. Keep things light and impersonal, right? That's what he wanted. But he missed her. He could picture her clearly in his mind. How fragile she'd looked when he'd found her lying in the snow on that mountain slope. He remembered in the lodge when he'd handed her a cup of chamomile tea and she'd gently blushed. He could not forget the sound of her laughter or the lilac scent of her shampoo. Remembering her refreshed him, when he had felt so weary. He sighed, dug down deep and began writing the truth.

On the surface, it was a great trip home. I had a blast joking with my brother, hanging out with my folks and being able to just breathe in the Wyoming air—there's nothing like it. I'd missed it like you wouldn't believe. Good memories were everywhere I went, everywhere I looked. Digging for arrowheads in the creek bank. Helping Skip haul in hay. Barbecues on the back patio. But beneath that, it was a tough trip, too. The family is no longer whole. There's a void no one can fill. There's a face missing at the table. A voice missing in our conversation. A laugh silenced that used to be the first to ring.

Giselle and Mom have the hardest time with Tim's loss. I'm doing all right, probably because I feel as if I carry on for him every day. It's what he wanted. I found myself borrowing Skip's truck and winding up at the cemetery. It was spitting snow. The wind was sharp and fierce. It made walking a misery, but I went to his grave anyhow. At the time on the street in Afghanistan, I did everything I knew to help him. After he fell, I had been the first one to reach him. I called for the corpsman. I checked for a pulse and started CPR. The ninety seconds or so that it took for a medic to reach us felt like a decade.

I kept up compressions, forgetting everything, the bullets, the grenades exploding. I didn't hear any of it. Just my pulse thundering in my ears and my prayers. Those were desperate prayers. I'd never prayed so hard in my life. Please let him live, I kept asking over and over. The corpsman told me it was about two minutes before Tim sputtered in air and we got a pulse. It felt like two centuries. I got hit by rock fragments when a bullet hit too close, and blood was streaming down my face—minor cuts—and I hadn't even noticed. When Oscar, the medic, peeled away Tim's flak jacket, he'd been hit twice in the chest near his heart. The two of us worked like mad to stabilize him, but he died in my arms. It was the toughest moment of my life. I'll always be grateful to God for giving us those few more minutes together. Tim and I said what needed to be said. I got to say goodbye to him.

There were things he told me, stuff I don't think everyone processed after the funeral. It was a rough time then. But I repeated his words to the family before I left. I think it helped them to hear again that Tim died without regret. Freedom isn't free. It comes at the price of lives unlived, so that others are free to live theirs. It's why I'll always be a soldier. Even if my career path takes me out of the field, I'll continue to serve this country however I can to the best of my ability. When I wear my uniform, I wear it for Tim, too.

That was more than you needed to know, huh? And I'm sorry for it. Talking about serious stuff is not my strong suit. But I feel better, so thanks for listening.

Later,

Pierce.

He sat in the half dark, debating about erasing most of the message. Was it too much? Too personal? Or would Lexie not want to hear about the real Pierce Granger? In the end he hit Send. The e-mail zipped off through cyberspace, too late to pull it back.

Lexie glanced up from the screen, surprised to find she was at a table on the second floor of the library with books spread out in front of her. She'd come by after her 8:00 a.m. class to keep searching for an elusive topic for her methods and stat paper. Instead, she'd checked her e-mail and had gotten caught up by Pierce's letter. His words still held a tight hold on her heart.

What he had been through. She hurt for him. More than anything, she wished she knew how to ease his sadness. There was only one thing she could think to do, so she bowed her head in prayer. *Father, please help him find peace, for he is a good man.*

Okay, so she was seriously crushing on Pierce Granger. Denial hadn't worked. Ignoring it wasn't working. She would simply have to accept the fact that she was sweet on him. There was nothing wrong with that, right?

Not really. They were friends, and nothing more was ever going to come of it. Her heart was safe, and what harm could come from having a high regard for a deserving friend?

She began to type.

Pierce,

Thank you for sharing your experience. It's heartbreaking, but I'm sure Tim is looking down on you from heaven and feeling proud of his big brother. It had to be a great comfort to him that you were with him in the end. Your family has paid a high price for this country. I am sorry for it, and I admire it.

Your growing-up experiences remind me so much of mine. Walking down to the creek on scorching hot summer days and sticking my bare feet in the cold, clear water. Having my grandparents over for Sunday barbecues with the briquette smoke and lighter fluid scent hovering in the air, mixing with charred hamburger. Popsicles cold and dripping on my hand as we sat in the backseat of the car with the windows rolled down because we had no air conditioner, bumping along the dirt road to town.

I love going back home. My aunt and uncle own the farm now. They took it over from Mom when Dad bugged out on us. Aunt Julie kept my horse for me. The only reason I could bear to leave Pogo was because I knew my aunt would take great care of him. I wish I could fly home on spring break (coming up next week), but I put in for extra shifts at the libe. Yes, you read that right. I'm spending spring break at the library. How did you know? Wait a minute, I'm afraid to know that answer. I'm sure it's not complimentary. I've always been a bookworm, and as my mother laments, I look like one, too. I'm not sure what that means, other than that I'm fairly quiet, but I'm afraid it means frumpy. Yikes.

What are you up to now that you're back on your base? How is the Seattle area rain treating you? What's the best part of your workday? What's one thing about you that no one would guess just by looking at you? Inquiring minds want to know!

Write when you can,

Lexie.

She waited for the letter to be sent, grateful for the safe life she had. It was a sheltered existence, considering other places in the world. The dozen or so library books sitting on the table no longer interested her. She had wandered through the stacks pulling out volumes on topics she was vaguely interested in for her thesis: eating disorders, suicide rates in teens, domestic abuse and family systems theory. But now, not so much.

Pierce had inspired her. She scooped up the books and dropped them on the nearby returns cart. Gathering up her things, she went in search of the card catalogue, excitement driving each step.

A frumpy bookworm? Lexie? Pierce hooted, the sound echoing in his tiny kitchen, and he took a big bite of pizza. A sausage rolled off and plopped onto the table, and he snapped that up, savoring it. Talk about starving. Every muscle he owned hurt—not bad, but enough to know he'd gone soft on his vacation. He chewed, set the slice back in the box, swiped his hands on a paper towel and started his return e-mail.

Lexie,

Forget any ideas of frumpy. Do you know what makes you look like a bookworm? It's that you're smart. Your mom has nothing to lament. Plenty of guys are looking for a smart, with-it kind of girl. You've got it going on. Which is why I can't believe you're spending so much time writing to a guy like me. I'm at least six notches beneath you on the with-it scale.

To answer your questions, I'm back to long days' training. Tonight we're expecting a training call. They always come in the middle of the night. Yes, it's raining for what has to be the millionth day in a row. At least it feels that way. I don't mind so much, except we've been spending so much time outside, I'm starting to grow moss. The best part of my workday is getting to break for lunch. C'mon, you knew my answer was going to revolve around food, right?

As far as the one thing no one would guess about me. Hmm, it's a toughie, but I think I'll surprise even you. I like museums. There's a flight museum not too far from here I go to now and then. I can even be dragged to art museums, but if you ask me in public, I'll deny knowing the difference between a Manet and a Monet.

Your turn. Tell me something no one else knows about you.

He stopped typing to finish off his slice of pizza, chomping away as he reread his letter. Maybe that was good enough. He could just hit Send and do his best not to think of her until her next note appeared in his in-box. But something held him back. There was a connection he couldn't deny, something that made him open up when he lived his life closed down. He went back to the keyboard.

For what you said about Tim, thanks. I got a call from Giselle last night, and there's been a change in her. She's hurting over Tim's loss, too, but at least she can talk about it now. She might not like my decision to stay in, but she isn't tortured by it. At least, it doesn't sound that way. I have you to thank. You helped her, and I'm grateful.

I've been put on notice, so who knows where I will be writing to you from next. Or when. If you don't hear from me for a while, it's nothing personal. I might not have Internet access. I'll catch you when I can.

Have fun on your wild spring break at the libe.

Pierce.

Pierce,

Here I am, writing to you on my wild spring break at the libe. Right now I'm at the check desk on the graduate wing, inspecting every book bag and backpack on the way out of the door. It's everyone's favorite job, because let's face it, the graduate wing of a small university isn't too hoppin'. It's the perfect spot for letter reading and writing. I hope this still finds you stateside. You have to be a little bummed that you might have to deploy right after you've gotten back.

Monet, huh? I didn't see that coming. I have a fondness for museums, too. When I was at MSU, I went to the Museum of the Rockies all the time. They have dinosaur exhibits. I like art museums, but no one will go with me because I take my time. When I went to Europe with my high school church group, I drove everyone nuts because I was always trailing waaay behind. I just wanted to soak in the beauty of the details. I've always wanted to go spend, like, two months at the Louvre, poking from one pic to another. The trouble is, I can't find anyone to go with me. No one I know wants to see that much of an art museum!

What's one thing about me that no one knows? I'm a jigsaw puzzle phenom. Okay, maybe not a phenom, but family members have banned puzzles from the house because I do them too fast. There, now it's your turn to tell a secret!

That's all for now from my wild life at the libe.

Blessings,

Lexie.

Lexie,

This is coming to you from an Asian country I can't name. I'm grabbing some computer time before we head out on an op I can't tell you about.

I never would have pegged you for a jigsaw genius. Who knew we had this in common, too? I like the huge ones that take up a whole tabletop. When we were kids, we would always have one going in the living room. It's a Granger family thing. I'm no jigsaw slouch, but it sounds like I can't hold a candle to you.

Another secret talent of mine: chess. I was captain of my high school chess club two years running. Your turn for a secret. I'll be waiting.

And hey, if you ever need a pokey art museum partner, I'll volunteer for the job. Not that I have much free time, but you never know.

Later,
Pierce.

Pierce,

I'll keep you in mind if I ever make it to Paris. Right now, I'm having a hard time budgeting change for laundry. It's a sign that I'm nearing the last quarter of the school year. Good thing I have a big paycheck coming from all those hours at spring break!

I can picture you as a chess champion—quiet, charming and strategic. I've been known to play a good game, but I'm out of practice. I would be no match for you.

A secret talent? I can pop a bag of microwave popcorn so that nearly every kernel pops without scorching it.

Your turn,
Lexie.

Lexie,

I'm seriously talented at eating popcorn, kernels and all. Right now I'm trying to ignore the guys who have just discovered I'm e-mailing you, a girl. I'm taking a ribbing. It's not easy being me.

Gotta run,
Pierce.

Pierce,

Sorry you have it so tough and that no one understands you.

Lexie.

Lexie,

I appreciate your sympathy. After much explanation and a water balloon fight, where I was victorious, I think I have finally made my fellow team members understand our relationship. That's another secret talent of mine. I am a water balloon champion. It dates back to the days when I was tormenting my little brothers on those hot Wyoming summer days. Not that I'm the kind of guy to torment anyone, but a big brother has his responsibilities.

Pierce.

Pierce,

I am not at all surprised to learn about your water balloon talents. I'm an only child, so my water balloon skills were never fully developed since I lacked adequate targets. Although I have some experience from when I spent parts of the summer with my cousins. I am much better at sprinkler hopping. Even now, I've been known to jump through a sprinkler and embarrass my mother. They live on a very hoity-toity street where girls in college are not usually seen running through lawn sprinklers.

I am running out of secret talents. One thing I'm really good at is making cake disappear. They had red velvet cake with cream cheese frosting for dessert at the dining hall, and I ate two pieces. Scary, but true.

Here's hoping that I'm not too dull for words, having gone through all my talents, and that you aren't bored beyond belief.

Take care,

Lexie.

Lexie glanced at her clock. She had five minutes to find her Bible. Now where was it hiding? As she clunked around her front room in her walking cast, she looked under cushions and behind pillows and beneath the piles of paper that seemed to be everywhere. Some of the sheets were class notes, others drafts of papers that were due, and some were just stuff she still had to deal with, like the appointment she needed to make with her faculty advisor.

Where could it be? She'd had it for morning chapel and it had been in her backpack at lunch when she'd wanted to look up a passage. What if she'd left it in the dining hall? Surely someone had turned it in to the lost and found bin, but she really didn't have time to go down and look for it. No, she'd had it when she'd looked up a passage for her religion class.

She sat down at her desk, deciding to plow through the stacks of paper and books one more time. Was it her fault her laptop was sitting there? She couldn't help tapping on the keyboard. It would take only a sec to check her in-box. It had been eight days since she'd sent her last e-mail to Pierce. Spring break was over and the last quarter of the school year had begun.

Why was her heart tapping like reveille as she waited for a peek at her messages? It defied explanation. She only knew that his name was not in her in-box. He hadn't written. Maybe he hadn't found time to, but that didn't change a disturbing truth.

She missed him. More than she wanted to admit.

"Lexie?" There was a rap at her door. Amber, Giselle and Rose were waiting for her, study books and Bibles in hand. "Are you ready?"

She closed her laptop and there was her Bible. The screen had been a good shield. She grabbed it, doing her best to put all thoughts of Pierce on hold. But those thoughts followed her as she grabbed her keys and stepped into the hallway. Her feelings for him stuck with her wherever she went.

Chapter Nine

It felt good to be back at base camp. Engines from the birds rumbled on takeoff like an earthquake through the mess tent as Pierce shoveled in the last bite of spaghetti and meatballs and tossed his fork on his tray. The tables were crammed with soldiers, which meant he might have a short wait for the computers. Still chewing, he grabbed his tray, bussed it and dashed through the pounding rain.

Beyond the secure perimeter of fence, razor wire and barriers was an unfamiliar landscape of dense jungle and low-topped mountains. Inside the perimeter was the familiar tent base that seemed unchanging. He hiked past tents offering glimpses inside of soldiers cleaning their rifles, reading or in heated, good-natured debates. Others hustled back and forth on duty. Dogs and their keepers patrolled the camp. Wing lights lifted through the sky as another transport took off.

He ducked into a tent, dripping with rain. He'd guessed right. Not only was there no line, but one of the computers was open. Hot dog! He dropped into the chair and began tapping away.

His excitement to hear from her had to be wrong. Why wasn't a warning bell going off in the back of his head? The bell that should remind him he was getting way too involved. There was no time for a warning of any kind, he realized, because he'd already spotted Lexie's e-mail waiting for him. It was too late. Logic set in. He told himself it wasn't a romantic interest. Lexie was an important link with normal life. But that didn't explain why he fidgeted impatiently while the computer took forever to open the letter. And it didn't explain why he'd bypassed reading other e-mails from Giselle, Sean and his uncle to open Lexie's first.

He read her words, hearing her voice and her intonation. Time and distance melted away and in his mind he was back on that campus with her, watching her smile sweeten her already adorable face and breathe to life something good inside him. The rigors of his deployment dissolved. He felt better than he had in a long time.

Lexie,

Me, bored by you? Never. This is the first time I've been able to sit down at a keyboard. They've got us pretty busy. When there's a natural disaster, someone has to help keep the peace if necessary. I got spoiled hanging out with you and with my family. It's easy to forget how easy I have things, because it doesn't seem easy at all. Back home I was worried about my family and their pressure to get out of the Army.

But all it takes is a week seeing villagers who have lost what little they have to remember my troubles are nothing. I'm reminded how blessed I've been all my life. I'm glad I've signed on the dotted line, and it's official. I'm in for another four years. It feels right.

My number-one blessing is good family and
friends. And yes, I guess that includes you. Although
don't quote me on that.

He leaned back in the chair, finger hovering over the
backspace key, debating those words. They looked stark
and final on the screen, as if they were more significant
than they were. If he sent it as it was, would Lexie read
something into it? Or would she understand how affirm-
ing it felt to be able to talk to her like this?

He was grateful for her friendship. She was on his
prayer list every night. Just writing to her made the exhaustion of his mission ease and the hardship of being
deployed only a minor blip. Yeah, he would leave it. He
trusted her to understand. He sat up and finished typing.

What's at the top of your blessing list?
I'll write when I can,
Pierce.

"Hey, Lexie."

At the whispered sound of her name, she blinked,
pulling herself out of Pierce's letter. She was in the library, studying at her favorite cubby in the far back
corner. Her classmate and friend, Cari, was standing
next to her desk, laden down with an armload of textbooks. She had a similar stack next to her computer.
"You look as exhausted as I feel."

"I keep hearing from my mom how much fun she had
in college." Cari rolled her eyes. "Where's the fun? I'm
missing it."

"Me, too. For me, it's mostly studying, writing tons
of papers and test anxiety."

"Yep, that's it exactly." Cari gave her long hair a toss and dropped her books on the window ledge. "How's your research paper going? Did you get your topic approved?"

"Yeah, but it was a shocker." She had decided on studying grief in military families. "I thought Dr. Fleming was going to nix it, but she loved it. It's too broad right now, but I'll get it focused."

"Cool. I had to revise mine. No surprise there." Cari gestured down the aisle. "I'm going down to the candy shop. Did you want me to get you anything?"

"I would love some chocolate." Not that she needed any. But did that stop her from digging out enough change for a Snickers bar? No. "Thanks, Cari."

"Hey, you did the same for me last week." She took the quarters, pocketed them, and gathered up her load of books. "I'll be back in a few."

Yes, she was grateful for the blessings of her friends, too. She considered the e-mail staring back at her on her screen. Seeing his answer and that he was fine made her glow like a moonbeam.

Pierce,

I'm glad to see a note from you in my in-box. I knew you were okay or Giselle would have told me, but still. A girl worries about her friends.

You've been peacekeeping, huh? There have been a couple natural disasters in the news—a tsunami and a drought that has driven people from their homes in search of food. I'm going to pay attention to the news tonight and think of you. You should be proud of the work you do. I am proud of you.

That said, now I feel almost guilty for how easy

my life is. You've got me thinking, Pierce. My biggest concerns are hitting my deadline schedule for my research project, getting ready for my brain biology and behavior test and being fairly frugal so that my spending money lasts until summer break. I don't have to worry about starvation or shelter or losing everything I've ever worked for. I've got it great in comparison. I know that and I'm grateful. I'm more determined to make good use of my opportunities. It would be wrong to waste them, when others don't have the same chances. That's at the top of my blessings list.

That said, I really should study, but what am I doing? Yes, I'm still writing to you. :) I count you in with some of my best blessings. It's rare to have a friend like you. I feel I can say anything to you. Maybe because you are so far away. Or maybe it's because we're more alike than we are different, like true kindred spirits.

Adios,

Lexie.

"One Snickers bar." Cari slid the candy on the desk. "You're not doing homework. You're writing a love letter."

"A *like* letter." She should have been listening for her friend's footsteps, but she'd been absorbed in her writing. "Really, it's even more of a crush letter, if that's possible."

"A crush letter? You mean you think wow about the guy, but he's not a keeper."

"Something like that." She reached for the candy bar and ripped the end off the wrapper. She couldn't imagine that Pierce would let anyone keep him. He'd sounded pretty adamant, for practical reasons and personal ones, which she could understand. It would be hard to have anything more than a friendship with so much of the world between them.

"It's nothing serious." She peeled the chocolate coating off the end of the bar and popped it into her mouth. "At least that's what I keep telling myself."

"It's the guy I saw you with that day in the cafeteria. Sounds to me as if you're falling for him." Cari backed away with her Butterfinger bar in hand, toward her cubicle. "Maybe that should be my project. The difference between love and almost love."

"Something tells me our professor won't go for it."

"You're right. See you!" She gave a finger wave and disappeared around the corner.

The student on the other side of the aisle stared at her in disapproval. They had been whispering, but it probably had been disruptive.

"Sorry," she said and went back to her computer, staring at the "message sent" note on her screen. It was in Pierce's in-box right now, wherever he was, safe or in danger. Her heart squeezed hard.

I'm not falling for him, she told herself firmly. But it was too late to stop the inevitable. She was falling for the dream of the guy, the stalwart soldier, the strong, good Christian man, the charming hunk that made her spirit as bright as the Milky Way.

She peeled another piece of chocolate off the candy bar, let it melt on her tongue and tried to focus her thoughts on her studying. It was impossible. It was too late for doom. She was heading straight for a serious disaster.

Lexie,

Nice thought, but kindred spirits is a girl thing. Guys do not have kindred spirits. We have buddies. Ranger Buddies. Army Buddies. Basic buddies. Tent buddies. FYI.

Another blessing I'm grateful for: dry socks. Seems like a small thing, sure, but when you've been wading through swamps and muddy ponds up to your waist and walking through the night rain in wet socks, you start longing for the simple comforts. A campfire. The chance to stand still for five minutes. Dry socks.

Your turn,

Pierce.

Pierce,

So sorry about the kindred spirits thing. I don't want to insult your male pride. I guess that puts me squarely in the homeland buddies category. :)

I have never realized the importance of dry socks, but I have to concur. I just got my walking cast off and wearing shoes and socks has never felt so good!

A blessing I'm grateful for: that time of night at the very end of your day, when everything is either done or you've let go of it because it has to wait until tomorrow. The night is quiet and still, and your prayers are said. That moment when I snuggle into bed ready to go to sleep is when I feel my most grateful. As if I am full from a day I've done my best with, and thankful for the chance to do it all again tomorrow.

Your bud,

Lexie.

Lexie,

Congrats on being a biped again. Mobility is a great thing. I'm guessing it's made your life a whole lot easier.

Sure, go ahead and rub it in. Some folks get a warm dry bed every night. We run a lot of missions at night. We're supposed to be prepping right now. I'm mostly done, but I wanted to jet off an e-mail to you before I go out. I'm suited and booted. Face paint is next. It's my favorite part, camouflaging my skin so I look like part of the terrain. Yeah, I know what's coming. Some joke about I'm already funny-looking enough as it is.

A blessing I'm grateful for: cheese sticks. Eat some for me the next time you get a chance.

Your bud,

Pierce.

Pierce,

I hope your mission went well and the face painting was as fulfilling as you hoped it would be.

I ate half a dozen cheesy sticks in your honor. It was pizza Friday at the dining hall, and I had more than a few slices of pizza, too.

A blessing I'm grateful for: long red licorice ropes. I'm pretending they have no calories, after all that pizza. Keep watching the mail because a surprise is on its way to you. It may or may not involve licorice ropes.

Summer is coming up and so is the leave you mentioned. If you're ready for a challenge, swing by my uncle's place on your way home. He's the only Evans in the Swinging Rope phone book.

Notice how I didn't make one comment about you being funny-looking?

Buds,

Lexie.

Was it wrong that she kept checking her e-mail? Lexie swallowed her disappointment. A week had gone by, and no answer from Pierce. She closed her in-box, turned her back on her computer and slipped out of her sweater. What was wrong with her? She scolded herself as she tossed her cardigan onto the sun-soaked arm of the sofa. She had a thousand things to do, with worship and school foremost, and yet what was topping her thoughts? Pierce's silence.

Stop worrying, she told herself. He's fine. He's gone longer than this without answering before. She dropped her keys on the corner of the desk and hefted her backpack from where it slumped, forgotten, on the floor. The problem wasn't Pierce's lack of response as much as it was with her. It was all her.

You can't deny it anymore, Alexis Anne Evans. You have more than a crush on the man. She dropped her pack on the sofa, plopped onto the cushion next to it and tugged on the zipper. Caring for Pierce had happened one small step at a time, so that she could try to ignore each step, but now that she looked over how far she'd come, she could see the flaw in her approach.

Ignoring her crush hadn't stopped it from growing. Treating her fond feelings as harmless hadn't stopped them from deepening. Her panic meter wasn't going off because he was half a world away and their only contact was through e-mail. Logically, there was no reason to panic. Nothing could come of their relationship. She knew that. It was one of the things that had been so attractive about their friendship.

But what was going to happen down the road? Was her affection for him going to continue to deepen? Would her heart be irrevocably broken?

A knock pounded on her partially open door, sending it swinging open. Amber stood frozen in the threshold, looking panicked. "Come quick! It's Giselle."

"Giselle?" She'd thought the girl was emotionally doing better, but everyone had bumps in the road. She followed Amber down the hall, her pulse frantic against her ribcage. Her ankle still twinged when she ran on it, but she raced anyway, passing opened doors giving views of girls studying at desks, on the floor with books strewn around them, on their beds, all very serious with finals a week away. A few were gathering up their things to head to lunch.

"I just turned on the TV to catch the noon news," Amber explained as she reached the end of the hall and the last door on the right. "And look what's on."

Giselle sat on the edge of her pink-covered bed, jaw dropped, eyes wide with terror, as pale as snow. She didn't blink, riveted to the small flat screen situated between their two desks where the caption on the ticker at the bottom of the screen rolled by like a headline. American embassy under siege. An Army helicopter shot down. Reports of casualties.

The air punched out of her lungs. Shock crept icily through her veins. Her knees buckled and she sank onto the bed. Helicopter down? It was unlikely Pierce would have been on it, right, although he was in that part of the country. She struggled for air, but there was nothing. Just the airlessness and the reporter's words echoing inside her head. "...Embassy is under attack. My sources tell me one of those choppers was carrying key American civilians on board. Heavy gunfire is reported from the area..."

"Th-that's where Pierce is. I'm sure of it." Giselle rasped, her whisper harsh with terror. "He's right in the middle of that. He's got to be."

"We can't know that for sure," Lexie found herself saying, not because she believed it, but because she wanted it to be true. She wanted nothing more in her entire life.

Lord, please let him be safe at his forward base, she prayed, with the sinking feeling it was an impossible request. She watched as the camera panned in the direction of a dusty brown and concrete city, framed by jungle-type vegetation. Orange flames shot up between buildings, and the pop-pop-pop of machine guns sounded like fireworks. The scene reminded her of a movie she saw where a Blackhawk was shot down, trapping soldiers in a hostile city.

Please keep him safe, Lord, she prayed with all of her might. She believed that prayer made all the difference, if there was one to be made. The image on the TV screen remained in the background, while the news anchor interviewed a former four-star general. She focused as hard as she could, but their conversation was a mumbling jumble she couldn't sort out. Her attention was on that image of flames rolling upward in the sky. That's where Pierce would be, right in the thick of things, defending the civilians he had probably helped rescue.

"I hate that he's there. I hate it." Giselle swiped at her tears.

"I do, too." Her hands trembled as she took Giselle's in her own. "But I'm proud of him, too."

"Will you stay with me?" A tear rolled down her cheek. "I can't wait through this alone."

"Absolutely. I wouldn't want to be anywhere else." If she could do this small thing by offering comfort to Pierce's sister, then she would do it. Her teeth chattered with fear for him, but she did her best to wrestle it down. "Do you want to pray for him? Will that help you?"

"I'd like that." Giselle sniffled, glancing once more at the screen. The TV had cut to another military expert, who was giving his opinion on the logistical difficulty of getting the wounded evacuated from the fighting.

Pierce was there, in harm's way. She knew it in her gut. A few moments ago she had been disappointed he hadn't had time to answer her. At the precise moment he'd been under attack. She could see why this was so hard for Giselle and her family, and for many of the military families at the nearby air base who had kindly completed her research questionnaire. She thought of some of their answers.

"It's stressful never knowing how my husband is, if he's safe and well. I jump whenever the doorbell rings," one Army wife had written. And another wrote, "I live in a constant state of worry. I've learned how to cope, but when you love someone you always want them to come home safely to you."

Lexie thought of those women now, and the thousands of families who sacrificed by supporting their loved ones on active duty. She could no longer pretend that she didn't care. The thought of Pierce possibly being hurt or worse cut her in two. As she bowed her head in prayer, one truth became perfectly clear. She was in love with him.

Chapter Ten

❧

"Reloading!" He bellowed out, ejecting his cartridge, dropping low. Cement bit into his knees.

Beside him, Hawk kept firing, calm and sure. Three embassy workers, a secretary, a consultant and a janitor, were trying to cope with the trauma behind them. A routine, peaceful evacuation had suddenly turned dangerous. The secretary and the consultant were weeping. The janitor, a stoic local, continuously recited the Lord's Prayer.

His prayers already said, Pierce palmed the magazine into his weapon with a familiar click. The concrete walls of the office building they'd stumbled in provided good cover and with the windows blown out, they had good defensive position near the downed bird.

"This was supposed to be a piece of cake," Hawk muttered. "Hey, Gray! Get on the horn and find out when our ride's coming."

"What do you think I've been doing?" Gray called out above the deafening explosion of an RPG.

Cement and shrapnel went flying, most of it missing

them. Good thing. He swiped dirt and cement dust from his face, struggling to see the helicopter wreckage and the injured copilot they were guarding. Jax was down, sprawled in the dirt and clutching his side, leaving a hole in the defense.

"Hawk, cover me." Pierce knocked Hawk in the arm. "I'm gonna get Jax."

Suppressive fire erupted behind him. He ran out through the spitting chunks of cement and whizzing bullets. The first step out into the open was the hardest. A man didn't have more than a chance to think of the people he loved before his boot hit the ground and he was exposed. It was Lexie's face that haunted him as he sprinted into the open, bullets pitting the earth around him.

The comforting scents of taco and seasoned beef filled the air as Amber set two dinner trays heaped with food from the dining hall onto the coffee table in Lexie's room. Giselle's support group had become too large for the smaller dorm room and they had been forced to relocate.

"I'm heading back for drinks." Amber surveyed the small crowd. "Who needs refills?"

"I'll have more iced tea. Thanks for all this, Amber." Lexie's stomach felt as if she'd swallowed a bucket of nails, but she managed what she hoped passed for a smile. "Giselle?"

The girl hardly seemed to notice. She was staring at the TV as if she hoped a journalist would come on and report Pierce's safety status. If only they could. Lexie took a plate from the tray and a napkin from the tidy stack. "Try to eat something, Giselle."

"I'm not hungry." Which is exactly what she said after Amber and Rose had fetched the first round of tacos from the dining hall.

"You have to eat something. This could go on for a long time." Right now the anchor discussed mortgage loans and the fed's speculated rate cut, and a very serious investment consultant doled out his view of things.

Worry ate at her. It was impossible to concentrate, except for the ticker at the bottom of the screen rolling around with the latest news tidbits. There had been no change in that, either, not where the military action was concerned.

"Pierce needs you to take care of yourself." She set the plate directly in front of Giselle. "Besides, I think there's statistical evidence that low blood sugar weakens prayer strength."

"You're making that up." The girl tore her gaze from the screen. "I'll try to get something down if you do."

"How can I say no to that?" Lexie took a plate for herself. The lush shredded lettuce, red juicy tomato, thick sour scream and melted cheese looked delicious in the corn taco shell, but the nails in her stomach seemed to have multiplied. She eased into her desk chair, put the plate on her knees and gathered a taco with both hands. One bite, and her stomach bunched up in protest. Giselle was watching, so she kept chewing.

The investment dude was still talking about T-bills, and she wished she could fast-forward live television to get to the part about the military action. What about the soldiers? Was it over? Were they out of harm's way? She had been praying for them all afternoon long, but it didn't feel as if it could ever be enough. Giselle had said that no news was good news. That was her only consolation now as she swallowed, and it was like swallowing sand.

She was totally getting the girl's view of things. No wonder she'd been so adamant about wanting Pierce out of the Army. It was one thing to look at his service in theory, terrifying to experience the reality of it.

But as nerve-racking as it was for her to wait, she couldn't imagine how tough it was for him. She did her best not to think about all the things that could go wrong. She could not bear to remember what he had said about being prepared to make the ultimate sacrifice. Her heart broke, and it took all her might to hold back the tears burning behind her eyes. She set her taco down, unable to take another bite.

Giselle's cell phone rang, and the girl jumped. Everyone jumped. Was it Mrs. Granger calling with unbearable news? Rose grabbed the remote and silenced the TV. The ticker tape rolled across the screen, "American embassy under siege. An Army helicopter shot down. Reports of casualties." Unchanged over the last hours. Was Pierce one of those casualties?

She went cold from the outside in while Giselle answered her phone, whispered "hello" and listened. One second turned into a century, two seconds into an eternity. She licked her dry lips, unable to feel anything, fearing what might be said, that Pierce had—

Don't think it, she instructed herself. He's got to be fine. He has to be.

"Oh, Mom." Giselle's bottom lip trembled. A tear rolled down her cheek. "I'm worried about him, too. A group of friends are watching a news channel with me. Yeah, I'm doing okay. We've had a prayer circle. I'm eating dinner, yes, I promise."

There was no bad news, simply a mother checking on her daughter. Relief rushed out of her like a tidal wave, knocking down every defense, every barrier, leaving her every vulnerability exposed.

I am in such trouble, she thought, resting her forehead in both hands. Every inch of her trembled. Her heart was too involved. Look at her, icy down to the soul in fear for him. Forgoing her studying seven days before finals because she couldn't focus on anything but worrying over Pierce and praying for his safety.

"Mom, they're talking about it right now. Wait." Giselle, phone in hand, turned her attention to the screen where the camera cut to a dark city street. The same correspondent was standing against a building, with the urban setting as a backdrop. Sporadic gunfire burst like a full bag of microwave popcorn, winding down.

Rose zipped the volume up.

"…fighting has stopped. There are still some insurgents in the area, but I can confirm the embassy is now evacuated and all American personnel are safe and accounted for."

The news anchor broke in, posing a question to some military analyst, and there was no news of more injured soldiers.

Thank You, Lord. The prayer lifted from the truest places in Lexie's soul.

"No news is good news," Giselle told everyone and returned to her conversation with her mom.

Lexie picked a tomato out of her taco and munched on it, feeling drained and in pieces. The feeling lasted through the night, into the following day and throughout the next week. As she answered essay questions on a blue book exam, writing about neurotransmitters, receptors and reuptake time, at the back of her mind the worry for him remained.

"Brownies!" Gray's victorious shout rose above the general chaos of their tent. The best thing about coming back from a tough mission was finding the letters and packages that had accumulated.

Pierce stared at his booty, a thick stack of letters, probably from Mom and Skip, who didn't want to fuss with e-mail, and a box from Lexie Evans. He sat on his cot, unable to make himself rip open the package.

"Have one." Gray tromped up, a shoebox of powdered sugar–topped brownies held out as an offering. "Layla made 'em. It's good to have a girlfriend."

Until she gets tired of waiting for you and leaves you for someone who isn't gone most of the time. He bit those words back. Maybe Gray would have better luck in the romance department. He took a brownie. "Tell Layla thanks."

"I will. Looks like you've got some goodies, too." Gray winked at him, as if the box was good news. He was young and still wet behind the ears. He hadn't felt the strain of what a demanding job meant to a man and his life back home. Gray tromped over to Hawk's cot, offering him a brownie, too.

That left Pierce to contemplate Lexie's box. He tore at the tape, taking his time, chewing on the brownie along the way. He didn't want to admit why he was dragging his feet. He didn't want to admit that his feelings for her were more than the simple friendship he'd agreed to.

If they were, he couldn't let them be.

"Looks like you made a good haul," Hawk commented as he opened a letter. "I can see the return addy from here. You and Lexie are still in contact?"

"Apparently." That was the safest answer. For how long, he didn't know. She was sure on his mind a lot. He'd gotten pretty personal in his e-mails to her—well, about as personal as a man like him was going to get. It had been simple opening up to her.

That was a sign right there.

"Aren't you going to open it?" Hawk prodded. "Maybe she sent cookies."

He was being wary, that was all, when he didn't need to be. Here he was worrying about his feelings getting beyond his comfort zone, when the truth was a girl like Lexie wanted a man she could count on. Someone who would be at her side every day. Jealousy ate at him as he imagined that lucky man, a guy who would be there for her, who could put her first.

Sadness crept into him, and as he tore at the last stubborn tape holding the box top together, it consumed him. He should be happy looking down at the treats she'd been thoughtful enough to send instead of being swamped with despair.

"Look at all that!" Hawk reached into the box and snagged a roll of sweet and tart candy. "You are one lucky dog."

"If only." He put his grin on, but he was about the unluckiest man in camp. "She's just being nice."

"I'll say. She's a nice girl." Hawk ripped open the paper wrapper and tossed a wafer into his mouth. He bit down, making a sour face. "It could work, you know. It's not ideal, but nothing ever is."

"I'm not looking to settle down." He grabbed a long strand of red licorice, wrapped in a long plastic sleeve, fighting to hide what hurt the most. With another job, under different circumstances, he might have a chance with her.

"Look at what Pierce got! Candy." Gray's call brought the rest of the team, rummaging through the selections for their own favorites. The guys gathered around him, hooting and teasing over their choices—grape bubble gum, rainbow-colored candies and peanut butter cups.

Pierce welcomed his buddies, gladly sharing and stealing a second rope before someone else could take it. The jokes and laughter helped him to forget his frustrations and the seeds of wishes he could not sow.

The chaos and noise was a happy sound, echoing in the hallway and into her room. The last finals were officially over and the students who hadn't bugged out yet were packing to go home. Christian music tumbled into the hallways along with laughter and tearful goodbyes.

Lexie opened her windows to the warm May breeze and soaked in the warm sunshine spilling through the leafy trees. She'd aced her final this morning, so the pressure was off. She only had to finish packing, get the last of the girls checked out of their rooms and pack the rest of her stuff into her SUV. Contentment filled her; it had been a good year, although the days had whipped by impossibly fast. All but the last seven. Those days had been torture.

She did her best to ignore her computer. She was *not* going to give in to the urge to check her e-mail for the umpteenth time. He would write when he could, just as he'd done before. Worry had turned into a dull ache, one nothing could ease.

"Lexie?" Giselle was at the door, her dark hair pulled back in a single ponytail, happiness on her face, sporting a yellow MCU T-shirt and tan walking shorts. "I'm on my way out and I wanted to see you one last time."

"I'm glad you did." She wove around the half-filled cardboard boxes to give the girl a hug. "I'm going to miss you, Giselle."

"Me, too." She pulled a tissue out of her pocket and swiped at her eyes. "Look at me. I'm a mess. I'm not good at goodbyes."

"It's not goodbye, it's I'll see you in a few months. With the way time is rolling by, it will be the last week of August before we know it, and we'll all be right back on campus. Besides, you can call or e-mail me anytime."

"I know." She sniffed and handed over her room key. "I'm going to pester you with e-mail. Just a warning."

"I'll look forward to it." She grabbed the clipboard from the edge of her desk and made a checkmark.

"By the way, I finally heard from Pierce." Giselle grabbed her purse and a heavy bag from the floor and hefted both over her shoulder.

"Pierce?" Her hands went cold. Everything did. "He's all right?"

"As right as he'll ever be, apparently." Giselle's shoulder slumped beneath the weight of her bags. "All that worry, and he's fine. He e-mailed me this morning. He's been keeping busy. No surprise there."

The ache deep in her heart sharpened. He was okay; of course she'd known that. No news was good news. Still, it was a relief to hear the words.

"I've got to get going. Mom wants me home by

supper, so she doesn't have to worry about me driving mountain roads in the dark."

"Drive safe, Giselle." She teared up, seeing the girl go. "Blessings."

"Blessings!" Giselle called back, hurrying down the hall, eager to get home.

Maybe there was an e-mail waiting for her, too. Images of Pierce teased Lexie as she dropped the clipboard on the coffee table and labeled the room key. She saw again the charm of his dimpled smile, the way he'd looked in the rain as he spoke about his brother, and how safe she'd felt in his arms when he'd carried her.

She found herself in front of her computer, impatiently waiting for the mail program to kick up. Tearful cries rang above the music and noise in the hallway and she glanced over her shoulder. Amber and Rose were hugging in farewell.

She blinked hard, willing down her emotions. A millennium passed before her mail program flashed onto the screen. She double-clicked, hands shaky, hungry to see his name on the screen, needing contact with him.

Her in-box was empty. No message from Pierce. Her hopes plummeted to the ground. She sank into the chair. He hadn't written her.

Her throat tightened, as if she'd swallowed a big ball of bread dough. It stuck there, stubbornly refusing to move as she stared at her screen. All the reasons why he hadn't e-mailed rolled through her head. He was busy, he only had time to write family, he had another mission, he was on his way back to the States. But her heart cracked in tiny, painful breaks because it knew the truth.

He had time to write to his family, but he hadn't made the same time for her.

With ice-cold fingers, she closed the program and shut down her computer. Time to pack it up anyway. She was down to her final three boxes, and then she would be checking out the last of the girls and heading home.

No joy touched her as she slid her laptop into its protective sleeve and placed it carefully in a box. The tiny breaks in her heart hurt as much as a huge one would have. She took a deep breath, grabbed the last can of orange soda from her fridge and popped the top. The cold liquid eked past the tightness in her throat.

So much for the safety of friendship. She set the can on her desk and went back to her packing.

Pierce stared at the screen, ignoring the sounds of PT drifting in from outside the tent. He'd waited in line to send a cheerful hello, and now that he was sitting at a keyboard the words didn't want to come. He shifted in the chair, ignoring the conversations rising and falling all around him from the soldiers at the phone banks or waiting in line for an opportunity to contact home.

Lexie,
One thing I'm grateful for: care packages. I devoured the licorice and the chocolate bars. Thanks. It was nice of you to think of me.

He stared at the words, shaking his head. He frowned, ignoring the knot of emotions cinched tight around his chest. It was all wrong. That wasn't what he wanted to say, not at all. He hit Delete and watched the words disappear. He tried again.

Lexie,

Sorry it took so long to get back to you. We ran into a little trouble on a mission. Nothing we couldn't handle. I hear from Giselle that you sat with her, held a prayer circle and gave her a lot of support. Thanks for that, and for the care package.

He stopped typing to read over what he'd written, gut tightening. No, this was all wrong, too. It didn't say what he really meant, how deeply it mattered to him that she had been there for his sister. He wanted to tell her how much her care package had meant, and the thoughtfulness behind it. That she would go to the trouble when her own life was so busy. He wanted to write how he'd ached from missing her e-mails on the long days he'd been away from base camp. And judging by all the emotions he was denying, he cared for her more than he wanted to admit.

Best not to analyze that too closely, right? Maybe he ought to go on typing, keep it easy, keep it light.

"What's takin' Granger so long?" Gray asked, standing behind him. "He's been sending a lot of e-mail since he got back from leave."

"Maybe he's got a girlfriend," Case speculated from the next computer over. "The candy girl."

"I'm not getting on that battlefield, remember?" Pierce started typing. "This is one man who isn't falling."

"Face it, Granger, even the strongest have to fall sometime." Gray sounded amused as he took a newly available chair at the end of the row. "Everyone has his match. It's hard to believe, but maybe you've met yours."

That was what he was scared of. He was a man of discipline, he prided himself on his self-control. But down deep he longed for her beautiful face, to see again the exact shade of blue of her eyes and the way they lit up when she laughed. It was a longing he had to deny.

He glanced around at the other soldiers keeping what contact they could with the ones who mattered. His guts cinched tighter. Denial was definitely the best choice. He didn't want to lose Lexie. It made no sense, but there it was. He hit Send, battling the words he'd left unsaid and the feelings unrecognized.

In her bedroom of her mom's house, Lexie stared at Pierce's e-mail.

I don't know what this summer will bring. Something tells me I may be stuck here for a while. If not and my plans change, I'll head your way. How's that?
Buds,
Pierce.

Buds. She couldn't make her eyes look at anything but that one word. Of course we are only friends, she told herself. She knew that. Just because her feelings had grown, that didn't change things between them. So why were the cracks in her heart expanding in depth and width? Why could she feel each tiny expansion like a fissure of pain through her soul?

"Lexie, honey?" Mom rapped on the open door.

She whipped out of her desk, mostly startled, but also not wanting her mother to see that she was down.

She pasted what she hoped would pass for an upbeat look on her face and went to take the laundry basket her mother was carrying. "Mom, you shouldn't be doing my laundry."

"It was in the dryer. All I did was fold it." Mom hovered in the nicest possible way. "I don't mind. I know you're busy up here. Oh, are you keeping in touch with a friend?"

There was that word again. "I didn't realize it had gotten so late. I'll come help you with supper."

"No need. The chicken is in the oven, the rice is on the stove and I've already made the salad. Len won't be home from work for a bit, so you may as well stay up here and answer your e-mail. I'm not even going to comment on the boy's name I see on the screen."

"Mother." Lexie rolled her eyes. Really. Time to change the subject before her mom started extolling the virtues of married life—this time around. "I need to finish packing my summer gear. I can't find my riding boots."

"Try the basement," Mom suggested, still hovering. "I know you're reluctant to date again, Lexie. I know Kevin hurt you."

"It was a long time ago, Mom." She wrapped her arms around her middle, hating that while that pain had passed, the memory had not. "I know all guys aren't like that."

"That's right. One day you will meet the right one." Mom came closer and brushed a lock of hair out of Lexie's eyes. "You make sure when you do, you risk your heart again. Life is too short to let what matters slip by."

Not exactly the advice she wanted to hear. Down deep, her feelings roiled, as if demanding recognition. On the surface, she could not talk about what hurt. She *had* found the right man—a trustworthy, honorable man straight out of her dreams. Except for one tiny problem—one huge, small thing. He didn't love her.

And never would.

"I'll call you when supper's ready."

"Thanks, Mom."

She waited until her mother was safely down the hall before she returned to her computer. With every crack in her heart stinging, she began to type. She did not tell Pierce how much she had missed his e-mails, or how often she thought about him and prayed for him. She did not mention her disappointment that his words had been impersonal or how she longed for the real Pierce Granger, for his quiet strength, manly tenderness and steadfast companionship.

Pierce,

I'm writing to you from my mom's place. School is over, finals are done (yay!) and I drive down to my aunt and uncle's tomorrow. I can't wait to see Pogo. The first thing I'm going to do is take him on a long, hot ride. Too bad you won't be able to join me. You're always welcome, but I get that you're a long way away and duty calls. Stay safe.

Your friend,

Lexie.

Friend. She stared at that word for a long time. She wanted more, knowing it was impossible. This was how it was going to be, their letters getting further apart and less personal over time. It wasn't what she wanted. She sent the letter into cyberspace, the cracks in her heart expanding with each painful beat.

Chapter Eleven

❧

Dust from the dirt road rose like a cloud, engulfing him as he angled the truck to a stop and studied the cluster of mailboxes. The names, if there had been any, had worn off long ago. A few of the boxes, victims of drive-by baseball bats, sported dents where numbers should have been.

He rolled down his window, ignoring the dust. Good thing finding his way with little direction was part of Ranger training, and growing up with country directions sure helped. The convenience store attendant in the little town of Swinging Rope ten miles back had advised, "When you hit the end of the county road, keep left until you see the mailboxes. The one shaped like a fish is Bill's. You'll know you're on the right road. Keep going until the stump, turn right and when you see the creek, it won't be far."

There was no fish-shaped mailbox. There was one painted like a trout, and it looked as if it had once sported a fin and a tail before being dented nearly in half. The dent looked recent, but the name on the side of the box was a casualty.

His instincts said to keep going. Pierce rolled up the window, swiped the dust from his face and caught movement in the field up ahead. His guts tightened. The back of his neck tingled. He knew it was her before his eyes could focus on the paint horse galloping through a field with a woman on its back.

Lexie. His soul stilled. Seeing her again made his troubles and conflicts fade into the background until there was only her. He took in her glossy hair as it whipped behind her, the kiss of a tan on her lovely face and the slender right ankle, which appeared completely healthy and healed. She looked beautiful and vibrant and happy.

Thank You, Lord. Gratitude filled him keenly, as if a physical pain. All the reasons he hadn't wanted to come were nothing compared to the glory of seeing her again.

Clinging to the back of her horse, she hadn't noticed him yet. She was riding into the sun, so she wouldn't see him until she was much closer. There was no bridle or saddle, just a lead tied to a halter as she bent close to the gelding's neck, the black mane whipping her face. Horse and rider streaked as one, flying low to the ground, wind lashing them and the sunshine blessing them.

She wore a yellow T-shirt, faded denim cutoffs and no shoes. He climbed out of the truck, leaving it idling in the summer heat. He tipped the brim of his Stetson as he crossed the road, kicking up chalky dust as he approached the fence. He knew the exact moment when she saw him. Surprise shifted across her face and joy sparkled in her eyes. He felt the impact of her emotion like a blow to his chest.

"Pierce! It's really you!" The horse changed direction,

dashing straight for the fence. The animal's gait slowed from gallop to trot and, with a skidding stop, closed the distance between them. The prettiest girl in the world slid off the back of that fine-looking bay paint and into the sweet wild grasses. She launched onto the bottom rung of the wood fence. "It's *so* great to see you! I can't believe you're here!"

Her arms flung around his neck, holding on before he could step away. His armor wasn't enough to protect him as he breathed in the summer scent of her, of wildflowers and sweetness. One thing he knew, she didn't belong in his arms. It was like winter holding hands with summer. Before he could draw back, she let go, flashing that dimpled smile at him, the one that made his heart forget to beat.

"Why didn't you tell me you were coming? I would have brushed my hair or something." She patted at the tousled mess of her hair, which wasn't messy at all, but perfect. Just like the rest of her.

His eyes drank up the sight of her. His spirit, as if thirsty for her nearness, leaned toward her. He had to force his boots to take a step back and put space between them, the safe distance reason demanded.

Maybe he had been a fool to come, he thought with a pang, but staying away had become impossible. He'd hated the long days spent trying not to think of her. Evenings that seemed empty without her e-mail to look forward to. He'd never written her back. He hadn't been able to.

"I should have called," he admitted. "This was part impulse and part opportunity. The powers that be sent us back to Fort Lewis, and since I had time coming I wanted to head home to Wyoming."

The whole truth: he'd wanted to come to her. Staying away had been too hard.

The horse reached over the fence, snuffling toward him so he held out his hand. Warm velvet lips and fine whiskers tickled his palm. "This must be Pogo?"

"The one and only. He was a wild mustang." She wrapped a lean, sun-browned arm around the gelding's neck. "When I was seven and totally horse-crazy, I begged my dad for a horse. We went to the bureau of land management's auction and I fell for this guy. It was love at first sight. He was a yearling, and I didn't know anything about a horse, but we managed."

"You gentled him and broke him to ride?"

"It was team work, mostly." One of the high points of her life had been those first years with Pogo, walking through the fields together, him following her hoping for bits of apples and cookies, popsicles or a taste of ice cream. "When Dad took off, it looked like I would have to sell Pogo. There was no money to care for him, not when it was all Mom could do to scrape together enough for our needs. If Aunt Julie hadn't offered to keep him for me, he would be someone else's best buddy right now."

"You must miss him during the school year."

"Horribly. I'm hoping after I finish my program next year, I'll be able to afford to keep him with me."

"In the city?"

"Who knows? I don't know where I'll land. I would like to have my own practice one day, but I'm flexible. I'll see where God leads me."

"There are riding stables in cities, too."

"Yes, so I'm sure the right thing will work out. It always does." At least that's what she told herself. She had to believe it. The fissures in her heart felt impossibly wide, but she was no longer hurting, not in his presence.

"That's what I tell myself, too." With the brim of his Stetson shading his face, he looked twice as handsome as she remembered. He braced both arms on the fence, striking a masculine and very Western pose. "It's good to see you again, Lexie."

"You're a sight for sore eyes, too." She shaded her eyes with her hand, savoring the look of him. His hard granite face and square jaw, the dimples flirting at the edges of his lopsided grin, and the charming confidence that made him stand out wherever he was, on a mountain top, in the rain, in sunshine. Longing filled her gently, purely, with the power of a thousand dreams.

The rough rumble of a small engine drowned out the lull of the wind and drew Pogo's attention. The mustang lifted his head, whinnying at the green front-load tractor rolling up the road—Uncle Bill coming in from the north field. He pulled to a stop behind Pierce's truck and hopped down.

"We got ourselves a traffic jam." Bill, in his ball cap, grass-dusted T-shirt and faded overalls, offered his hand. "You must be a friend of Lexie's."

"Yes, sir." The men shook hands, Pierce friendly, Bill carefully measuring the younger man.

"Pierce Granger is the one who rescued me on the mountain when I fell. I told you about that." She'd left out all the private details, like how blessed she felt to have met him, like how wonderfully protected it had been in his arms, and how bereft she was that he'd gone a month without writing. "You know all those e-mails I get from Giselle? She is his sister."

"I see." Bill took off his cap, letting the wind ruffle his salt-and-pepper hair. "Good to meet you, Pierce. It's a scorcher today. You come right on up to the house and have some of Julie's pink lemonade. It'll wet your whistle."

"Thanks, sir, I will."

"You Army, boy?"

"Thirty-seventh Ranger Battalion. You, sir?"

"Served two tours in Vietnam. Infantry." Bill nodded his approval. "I like you, boy. Now move your truck so I can get home."

That was her uncle, to the point with a grin on his face. Lexie grabbed Pogo's lead. "See you up at the house," she called.

As Pierce raised his hand in answer, striding into the slant of the sunlight, the world stopped turning. Just like it did the first time he'd taken her hand, everything within her stilled. Love seeped through the cracks, impossible to hold back. The connection forged between them remained, tensile and unyielding and impossible to deny.

Did he feel it, too? Was that why he was here? She swung onto Pogo's back, gripping a handful of mane, praying that she could hold on to what was left of her heart. Pierce was a bad heartbreak waiting to happen.

"Here you kids go." Julie Evans finished pouring a pitcher of lemonade into two tall glasses and set it on the cloth-covered patio table. "You holler if you need anything. Pierce, you're going to stay for supper."

He leaned back in the wrought-iron chair. He liked the woman with her to-the-point manner. It was clear she kept everything shipshape. "I don't want to impose."

"You won't be. Now, as long as we're all clear that you're staying, I'll get back to my gardening." She grabbed a straw hat from a wicker seat, dropped it on her head and pulled a pair of gardening gloves from her back jeans pocket. Her sneakers padded down the walkway, where tall stands of bold-colored flowers bloomed cheerfully.

"You passed muster." Across the umbrella-topped table, Lexie grabbed a cookie off the plate between them. "They like you."

"Those poor misguided folks." He gulped down a swallow of lemonade. Sweet and tart, just right. "I bet you're wondering what I'm doing here."

"Stopping by, obviously. You didn't write or call. Not that you had to." She stared down at her cookie, her emotions shielded to him. "I'm sure you were busy."

He could have made time. Truth was, he was afraid to. He didn't like that about himself. "I don't want you to think you were low on my priority list, because you weren't."

Her big blue eyes met his, shielded, just as he suspected his were. Man, she was a sight, her hair wind-blown, looking like beauty itself, her goodness shining through. His chest cinched up with longing that had nothing to do with friendship and everything to do with something richer.

"I understand." Her quiet words saved him. She wasn't going to make him explain. "Since that American embassy thing on the news, I've developed a different opinion about you."

"You have?" He reached for a chocolate cookie and took a bite. Soft and moist, he chewed, grateful because it gave him something to focus on. Something that seemed casual, sitting together in the shade on the back patio, surrounded by flowers and the tang of lemonade.

His interest in her answer was far from casual. What did she think about what he did, now that she had sat through the event with Giselle? Lexie could have no illusions about him. He carried a gun and used it, sparingly and defensively, but still, he used it. Did she think less of him?

"On the news reports there were all these people fleeing from the fighting. That I understand. I get running from danger." She took a dainty sip of lemonade and relaxed into the cushions. "It has to take a lot of courage to stay. What you do makes a difference. People are alive because of you and your fellow Rangers. I saw the interviews some of the embassy workers gave."

Talk about relief. He took a long swallow of icy lemonade because he didn't trust his voice. Her answer mattered more than he could measure; her answer had made things impossibly harder. If she didn't see the merit in his work, if her views of him had changed, then ending this and walking away would be a thousand times easier. Enduring her endearing ways and honest goodness was going to be a million times harder.

Hot wind puffed against his face as he set the glass down. He'd drained every drop. Before he could reach for the pitcher, Lexie lifted it from the table, leaned closer with her lilacs and summer breeze scent and poured.

"Your parents must have been glad to see you." She set the pitcher down, her question a small one. The question in her eyes was a much bigger deal.

"I haven't been to see my parents yet." It was impossible to explain. He should have stopped by to see his family first, but instead he had driven straight to her. "I plan on seeing family next. I have thirty days coming. Hawk and I were going to head up to Alaska and do some sightseeing next week, but I had a hankering to see Wyoming again."

"So here you are." The question faded from her eyes.

"Here I am." Maybe she understood what he couldn't say. What he could never say. She had come to mean more to him than anything on this earth. He didn't have a clue how that had happened. Between carrying her in the snow and typing his last letter to her, everything had changed. Slowly, silently, gently. "I should have called."

"But you were on vacation, going where the wind took you?"

"Exactly." That tangled knot of feelings had led him here. There were important things he could not tell her, because they were too deep and vulnerable. Those feelings were not why he had come. He stole another chocolate cookie from the plate. "This is where you grew up?"

"I took my first step right there by the back door." She pointed to the patio where planter boxes brimmed with bold red and purple petunias. "There are a lot of good memories here."

"You must miss your mom. You don't see her during the summer?"

"I see her more when I'm here than when I'm in school." She didn't mention the calls back and forth and the weekend visits. Pierce hadn't come to hear about her family's travel habits. She didn't know what else to say. She couldn't ask him what she truly wanted to. She couldn't say what really mattered. She took another cookie, not at all sure what to do, grateful when he broke the silence.

"I've missed you more than I wanted to." His voice dipped low. He stared hard at the woven green tablecloth. "More than I realized."

That surprised her. "When I saw you at the fence line, I couldn't believe my eyes. I m-missed you, too."

That was incredibly hard to say. She squirmed in the chair, wanting to get up and dart away until she felt more comfortable. Until her heart was safe.

"I wanted to see you. And now that I have—" He avoided her, staring across the lush green lawn to the orderly rows of the vegetable garden. Julie sat on a little wooden stool, thinning carrots. He gazed farther out, as if trying to find an answer on the mountain-rimmed horizon. "I can't stay long. But maybe long enough for that horse ride you threatened me with."

"Great. We have a green broke horse that will be a real challenge." She could see his struggle. Was it like hers? Afraid to get close, afraid to let go? "You do like challenges, right?"

"Only when I won't wind up in the dirt, broken and bleeding. Some battles I stay away from." A muscle ticked in his jaw, betraying him.

She remembered what he had said long ago. *Love is one battlefield I want to stay off of.* His words swung at her like a silent, unseen mace, obliterating the tiny hope she didn't know was there. She set her chin, refusing to let him see it. Doing her best not to feel the cold sweep of pain washing through her. "Then you can ride Red. He's a gentle old soul."

"Gentle. I can handle that." Unaware of how he'd hurt her, he flashed her a grin, the one she loved so well.

His hazel eyes flashed green and gold and the dimples dug deep into his cheeks. "I've got a hotel room in town for a few days. That ought to be enough to see the sights around here, don't you think?"

"Especially if you don't mind hanging out while I do my chores. It's about time to start in the barn." She bopped to her feet, but didn't take a step, both needing to stay and to go. Retreating to the barn's warm shade and comforting animals seemed like the perfect solution. Best to put some distance between them. She didn't know how long she could keep her feelings buried. "If you want to hang here, I can get more cookies. Or you could take a walk around. There's TV inside. You could take a nap. I won't be long."

"I'll come with you." He stood, grabbing the pitcher and the cookie plate. "I have some experience with barn work."

"Some?" She grabbed the cups.

"Meaning a lot." He held open the door. "I'm not one to sit around when there's work to be done."

"You're on vacation." The tile was cool on her feet as she padded straight to the dishwasher and loaded the cups. "I don't expect you to pitch out stalls."

"It's one of my many talents." He left the cookies on the counter and the lemonade in the fridge. "Now don't go making jokes about my mucking-out capabilities. It's tempting, I know."

"I wasn't planning on saying a word." She grabbed her baseball cap from the peg on the wall. "I never turn down help filling the wheelbarrow."

"Mighty sensible of you. I know what goes in that wheelbarrow."

"Most animals are outside this time of year, so we're

lucky." She leaned against the door, opening it, trying her best to look everywhere but at him. Impossible. He filled the room. He filled her field of vision. She shoved open the door, stumbling onto the hot bite of cement and the day's baking heat.

She heard his gait behind her, felt his arm take the weight of the door and she launched away from him, determined to keep whatever space she could manage between them. But he fell in line beside her. They bypassed flower beds fragrant with colorful roses. It was a dazzling day with the sky as blue as dreams and the wild grasses singing lazily in the breeze. Horses grazed in verdant fields and shade trees dappled sunlight over them as they walked together, side by side.

There was no getting away from him. He stuck by her, towering at her side. "I wish I could stay longer."

"I understand. Alaska is waiting. It sounds fun." She pulled the bill of her cap lower to shade her eyes. "What are you guys going to do? Sightsee?"

"Mostly. Rumor is we're going to camp, canoe, fish for our own dinner."

"Ah, the stuff you think is fun, but really isn't?"

"That would be it. We've been planning it for the better part of a year." They were coming up on the barn, a big red structure opening out to the horse pasture. Pogo lifted his head to nicker at Lexie, then returned to his grazing. Pierce eyed several of the large animals. One was a sorrel, red from nose to tail. "That wouldn't happen to be Red?"

"That's him. Anxious to ride him?" She sparkled with mischief.

"You picked out the biggest one on purpose, didn't you?" Tomorrow was going to be interesting.

"I promise he's the gentlest one. That's the upside.

The downside would be that if you fall, it's a much longer distance to the ground." Grass whispered beneath her feet. "If you want to keep your boots nice, there's an extra set of Uncle Bill's boots. He won't mind if you borrow them."

"I just might, that way I don't track stable muck into your aunt's house." He followed her into the shadowed entrance of the barn, their movements rustling in the big silent structure. The haymow overhead was nearly empty of hay, but the sweet scent of it lingered as if freshly mown. The first cut wouldn't be brought in until after the fourth. A pair of chickadees cheeped overhead, warning the intruders of their domain.

He took the rubber barn boots from Lexie, and one lone calf bleated from somewhere inside the belly of the barn in one long low.

"That's Buffy. She's always the first—" She was drowned out by a bellow of bawling calf cries. She jammed her feet into barn boots and tugged them up. "I'm coming, babies. Hold on."

That only brought a bigger round of moos. Unaffected, Lexie led the way to a side room, where counters sported plastic milk bottles set out to dry and a deep double-sized sink. A fifty-pound bag of milk replacer sat by the cabinets, open, with a measuring scoop handle-up in the powder mix.

"Need any help?" His question brought an instant head shake from her.

"I've got this down to a science." She turned on the faucet, holding her hand under the stream, adjusting the taps for the right temperature.

"I won't mess up your system." He ambled next to

her and began righting the dozens of bottles on the counter. "How many calves?"

"Fifty-two. Let me guess. That's a small number to you. Your family has a bigger spread?"

"My folks only raise a few for beef. Now my uncle, he's got a big spread. I don't know how many calves they have in a year, but it's staggering." He watched as Lexie grabbed a five-gallon bucket and dropped it into the sink. A few huge scoops of milk replacer added to water, and stirred. He'd seen it before. Knowing the routine, he began lining the bottles into the sink while she checked for any lumps and kept stirring.

Something moved in the corner of his vision. A white streak plopped onto the counter and sat with feline grace. Two blue eyes studied him as the cat began licking one pristine paw.

"Snowball, meet Pierce." Lexie dropped the long handled spoon on the counter.

He grabbed the handle before she could. "Don't argue. I'm not about to stand here and let you lift this. It's heavy."

"I do it dozens of times a day."

"Not today." He began pouring, careful not to spill. "Tell me whoa."

"Whoa." She took the partially full bottle while he filled another to the same level. "Why didn't you write me?"

"Honest?" His pulse skidded to a rocky stop. He kept his hands steady, moving onto the next bottle. But out of the corner of his eye, he kept a careful watch on her.

"Yes, I want the whole truth." She topped the bottle and set it on the counter. Vulnerable. It was in the wide guilelessness of her eye. He remembered what she had told him, how hurt she'd been by love.

No miles separated them, this was face-to-face, without time and distance making it easier to keep it light. There was no computer screen to hide behind. He filled the last bottle in the sink and set the bucket on the counter.

Maybe it was time to be no-holds-barred and armor off. "I didn't write because I was afraid to. You've gotten too close to me, Lexie."

"I feel the same way," she agreed.

"Distance is safer." He didn't know why he could read the emotions on her face, he'd never been able to see anyone so much. Understanding, fear, agreement, it was all right there between them.

They worked together, topping bottles, as the calves bawled soulfully.

"What are we going to do about it?" she asked.

"I don't know." He finished the last bottle in the sink, handed it to her, and their fingers brushed. The simple contact felt like a tsunami's leading edge hitting him, obliterating him, carrying him out to sea. He pulled away and gathered half of the bottles, working methodically, keeping his emotions on hold.

"The babies are waiting." She gathered the bottles in her arms and led the way down the far aisle, the cat trailing after her.

The words he'd spoken were between them now, a truth neither of them knew what to do with. As he followed her, he couldn't help thinking it was like driving down an unexplored road in a Humvee and knowing in an instant before you were ready to drive over an IED. Knowing that after the boom, nothing would be whole again. You wouldn't be whole again.

A smart man would stop if he could.

"What is all this fuss about?" Lexie's gentle voice rose above the rustle and cries of the calves, penned two to a stall. She set the extra bottles on a nearby shelf, talking all the while.

He caught a glimpse of snowy white noses and velvet red coats between the gate rungs as the little ones stretched as far as they could toward their caretaker.

"Buffy and Button, you're first." She cradled the bottles, one in each arm, holding them for the calves. Hungry mouths latched on, big brown eyes watching her with adoration. "What good girls you are. Now, you boys, you wait your turn. Ladies first."

The hungry calves in the other pens bawled, begging for Lexie's attention and a warm bottle. Light sifted down from the haymow, gracing her, and Pierce froze in the aisle, awed by this new side of her. She had been the stoic injured girl in his arms, the understanding friend he could confide in, the lovely graduate student at the symphony, the smart and fun pen pal, the sun-kissed woman riding her horse bareback through a field, and now this, the country girl bottle-feeding two calves.

It was more than his heart could take. He fell hard and so far in love with her, he would never be whole again.

Chapter Twelve

The evening had been flawless. Uncle Bill's barbecued bacon burgers and Aunt Julie's potato salad and fixings had been the perfect complement to the pleasant afternoon. Followed by chocolate cream pie, cold sweet tea and a hot, lazy sunset. At the moment Lexie couldn't ask for more.

On the patio watching the riot of purple, magenta and gold paint the horizon, she couldn't measure her contentment. It seemed limitless. With her feet up on the ottoman, leaning back in the comfy chair cushions with Pierce at her side, she felt life couldn't get any better. It simply couldn't. It didn't seem possible.

"Yep, this is the best place to be, in my opinion." Uncle Bill pulled out a chair and took a seat, setting his glass of tea on the table. "Every now and then I get the notion to go traveling, but I never get farther than this."

"Why would you?" Pierce agreed, the ice in his glass tinkling as he took a sip. "I've seen a fair part of the world and I've never seen anything as peaceful as those Wyoming mountains."

"I believe you, son. I did my traveling in my Army days, and I don't miss it."

"Speak for yourself," Aunt Julie piped up from the railing, where she was lighting a citronella candle. "I didn't have any Army days. I, for one, would like to see more than my backyard."

"Come over here and I'll change your mind." Bill winked and patted the chair beside him, as if knowing full well that would make his wife chuckle warmly. "Lexie, how about you? Do you want to see the world?"

"I'm not opposed to it, but I don't feel like I have to, either." She took a sip of tea and savored the sweetness. "Basically, I can be happy wherever I am."

Beside her she felt Pierce's intense scrutiny. He'd been like that since he'd fed the animals with her. First holding the bottles for the calves, the dear little things, as they butted and bawled and craved affection. He'd been an old pro at feeding grain, handling the calves with care and cleaning out their pens. He'd good-naturedly helped her feed and water the rest of the stock and horses.

What was he thinking? She stared out at the stunning sunset, where the blinding blaze of the sun slipped farther behind the mountains, but the scene no longer calmed her. Pierce wasn't looking for serious; she knew that. But did he regret coming? Was this all too mundane for him? Was he thinking, who knew a girl could be so provincial and boring? He lived an adventurous life. Yet another reason why it would never work between them.

"I would be happy seeing Paris once in my life." Julie winked as she pocketed the matches and tapped across the patio to her husband's waiting arms. "Or the Great Barrier Reef. I would like to see that. I've always wanted to snorkel."

"I'll take you over to the pond then, and we can see what's under the lily pads," Bill teased, love warm in his voice.

"Oh, you!" Julie laughed, slipping out of his hug. "I've seen enough frogs. While you're here, Pierce, you should have Lexie take you up along the creek. There's a swimming hole not too far from here. I'll make you two a nice picnic lunch to take along."

"That sounds real fine, ma'am." Pierce stretched out in the chaise beside her, appeared interested. "There's nothing like a cool dip on a hot day. I don't want to put you to any trouble."

"I'm used to trouble," Julie assured him.

"I am, too," Lexie spoke up, fully intending to help with any preparations. The thing was, she knew Pierce well enough to recognize the tiny crinkles around his eyes, a sign of strain. *I didn't write because I was afraid to,* he'd said. *You've gotten too close to me, Lexie.*

He didn't want to be too close to her. Maybe to anyone. She had that much figured out. She didn't want anyone too close to her, either, and look what had happened. Love blazed in her hurting heart with colors and shades she had never known before and so brightly, he was all she could see. The world faded, the birdsong and breeze silenced until there was only Pierce and dreams of him she refused to let bloom. Dreams of wedding vows, of children and happily ever after that she could not allow.

"You're going to expect me to ride a horse to the swimming hole, aren't you?" Pierce was saying. "This is going to be interesting."

"Don't you ride?" Bill asked.

The breeze gusted lazily in a hot, grass-scented puff,

and a deer with twin fawns ambled out of the field and onto the lawn, watching them with wary eyes before getting back to the business of grazing.

"No," Pierce answered. "Now, in case Lexie is pulling my leg, I want you two to verify that the big horse named Red is in fact tame."

"As gentle as a kitten," Julie assured him. "Do you know how to ride?"

"My experience is mostly in falling."

That made everyone laugh, as he figured it might. His glass was empty, the sun was fully down, leaving a last haze of daylight that was bound to quickly drain away. He climbed to his feet. "I hate to say it, but it's time to go."

"I do wish you would stay with us." Julie seemed genuinely troubled. "It would save you the cost of a hotel, and those rooms are never as comfortable as a home."

"I'm comfortable enough." That was one thing about deployment. You learned to appreciate the basics of life, and he had learned he didn't need much. "Besides, I don't want to put you folks to any trouble. Thanks again for supper. It was mighty tasty."

"Anytime, Pierce. Don't you forget that."

"See you in the morning, son." Bill stood to shake his hand. A good, firm grip, callused from a life of hard honest work. "If you want a more challenging mount, you let me know and I'll saddle up Tasmanian for you."

"Uh, thanks, but no thanks. Good night." He didn't want to break away; at the same time his gut was telling him to go. Lexie may have faded into the background for a moment, but he couldn't forget her. Her nearness affected him. The back of his neck tingled. The tangle of emotions bound up in his chest until he couldn't breathe.

Her bare feet whispered behind him in the grass as he circled around the house. He'd done his best not to look at her directly since the barn, but he couldn't go back and change his revelation. He couldn't undo his affection any more than he could reverse time. When he reached the edge of the lawn, where grass gave way to gravel and his rental truck was parked in the shade of the house, he gathered his reserves before facing her.

"Julie means well." Apology made her eyes a deeper shade of blue, and the emotion on her pretty face was unveiled, plain for him to see. "She only wants you to have a good visit, but I don't want you to feel obligated to come tomorrow or to spend the day swimming in the creek."

"Obligated? That's not the word I would use." Try lucky. Glad. Worried. The last twinges of daylight fell between them like hope, like opportunity, and in the soft light, she had never looked more beautiful. His soul ached for her. He savored the look of her long, curled eyelashes framing her perfect blue eyes, her exquisitely cut cheekbones and darling slope of her nose, her rose petal–soft mouth and the smile that curved upward in the corners.

Love, powerful and pure, thumped like a cluster bomb through his chest, driving out fear and doubt and every drop of lonesomeness. He felt whole, when he hadn't known anything was missing until now, until this moment. He wanted to draw her into his arms and never let go.

"It was my plan to spend the day with you." His voice sounded rough and raw, as if too much of his emotions had made it past his armor. He straightened his shoulders, drawing up all his might. Whatever his love for her, he could not let it show. "I'll even get on a horse. That's saying a lot right there."

"You're just lucky I can fit you into my hectic, demanding schedule." Her words were lighthearted, her grin sweet, but her eyes were veiled. As twilight crept over the land, soaking into the shadows, it hid the tiny hints of truth on her face.

But he could see deeper. He felt her vulnerability and fears as greatly as he felt his own.

"Yeah," he joked, choosing to keep things lights, too, where they were both comfortable. "I saw those calves. Very demanding."

"I'm glad it's not haying season yet, or I wouldn't be able to get away."

"I wouldn't mind helping out in the field." As long as he could be with her. He would go anywhere and do anything for her. Commitment filled him, unbidden and unexpected, protective and strong. Love for her hurt with brutal force, and he took a step back, struggling to keep the safe wall of friendship firmly between them. He tugged his keys from his jeans pocket. "I'll see you tomorrow. What time?"

"Any time you want. You're the one on vacation. You shouldn't have to be anywhere on time. Come when you can." The breeze ruffled the dark curtain of her hair, and as twilight deepened and the first stars of the night shone in the gray sky behind her, he wanted to kiss her. More than life itself, he wanted to cradle her chin in his hands, gaze into her eyes until his soul sighed and kiss her with all the tenderness he owned.

Good thing he was smart enough to leave before he

could. His boots crunched in the gravel as he circled around the truck, but as he climbed into the cab, distance gave him no relief. Tenderness left him dizzy as he started the engine.

When he drove away, he kept sight of her in the mirror. She stood at the edge of the driveway watching him go. Framed by stars and mountains, she looked like the ideal image of a wholesome country girl in her simple T-shirt and cutoffs, but she was much more.

She was his heart.

"Pierce is a nice boy." Aunt Julie snapped the lid closed on thick pieces of gingerbread cake the next morning. "Of course, he *is* from Wyoming."

"That makes all the difference." Tongue in cheek, Lexie carefully wedged the plastic container into the bulging saddle pack. "He's only a friend."

"I wasn't saying any different." Julie covered the cake pan and carried it to the counter. "You ought to invite him to church with us tomorrow."

"I was planning on it." Oh, she knew where her aunt was going with this, bless her. "Remember I said he was a friend?"

"I heard it loud and clear." Her twinkling eyes said otherwise. "Whatever you need to tell yourself, honey, but I can see the truth as plain as day."

"Truth? There is no truth." None that counted, anyway. All the love in the world wouldn't make Pierce stay. He had four more years in the Army, and she had a degree to finish. Just one more reason she had to keep a tight rein on her heart. "Neither of us wants anything serious."

"Fine. Use any excuse you want, but you love the boy."

To deny it would be a lie. Lexie grabbed a tube of sunscreen and slipped it into the pack's outside pocket.

"I thought so. He's in love with you, too."

"No, that's impossible." She methodically hooked her sunglasses into her T-shirt's collar. She kept her feelings very still, but a small hope heard those words and stirred. She tugged her gray Stetson from the hooks. "He's a loner of a guy and he likes it that way."

"Okay, fine." Julie leaned over the sink to get a good look at the driver. "Then Mr. Lone Wolf is driving up at nine forty-three on a Saturday morning. Could mean he's eager to see you."

That small hope buried inside her stirred again. Quelling it, she lifted the pack and swung it onto her shoulder. "Or it could mean he's an early riser, too, which he is. He knows I get up at four-thirty to feed the calves."

"All right. You know best." Julie's wide grin said otherwise. "You kids have fun. Watch out for that cougar we've been having trouble with. You've got the two-way just in case?"

"I got it." She grabbed it on the way out the door and hooked it into the pocket of her pack. "I'll be back for the chores. See you then!"

"Bye, sweetie."

Lexie shut the door, unaware of the weight of the bag or how quick she circled the house. It wasn't as if she was anxious to see him again, really. That couldn't be the reason her feet were carrying her through the gravel toward him. It had to be the wind at her back pushing her along, instead of her heart pulling her.

"Hey, sunshine." Pierce strolled toward her, lowering his aviator sunglasses. He wore an olive-green

T-shirt, cutoffs, and a camouflage cap, looking like he was ready for a summer outing.

Seeing him was like peace touching her soul, like hope dawning, all her dreams coming to life. Those sensible, logical reasons why she had to resist hoping silenced. Not smart, it wasn't logical. It was emotional.

"You look ready to hit the trail. I've been talking myself into it all morning." He stopped to yank a small duffel from the bed of the truck. "I'm mentally prepared for the mission ahead."

"You have nothing to worry about. It will be fun. Maybe not as fun as racing down the mountain shouting 'banzai', but fun."

"No racing." He grinned, looking fairly adamant about that. He hefted the saddlebag from her shoulder before she could protest. "Usually I like speed, but when I'm on the back of a horse, not so much."

"Got it. We'll keep it to a safe trot."

"Hey, I know about trotting. No trotting."

"You don't want to bounce around in the saddle?"

"Bounce, slap, fall off. No, miss, I do not." Chuckling, he fell in beside her, their gait in sync. "Is this an all-day mission?"

"That's the plan, except I have to be back at four-thirty to do my chores."

"Suits me fine. I figure we'll come back, get the barn work done together and then the two of us can hit town. I noticed there is a street fair going on."

"Swinging Rope Founder Days. I've been meaning to go." A lock of hair tumbled down from her hat, which framed her face adorably. "There's a rodeo tonight."

"Yep, thought we could catch it." Casual, that's how he had to keep it, although that didn't explain why his palms had gone damp. It might be because of the heat, but more likely because being with her mattered. "Okay?"

"Okay."

They'd reached the barn, where light filtered from the haymow where the white cat was sitting, staring regally at him. Two horses were cross-tied in the aisle, saddled and ready. Pogo lifted his head, nickering in greeting, glad to see his owner. The big animal turned to putty as he lowered his nose for Lexie's affectionate touch.

Pretty lucky horse, to Pierce's way of thinking, to mean so much to her. He took a step back, drawing the red giant's attention. The gelding studied him with measuring eyes, as if he had already figured out who would be riding him and how to keep the upper hand.

Great. All he could do was to hope for the best and that he didn't end up on his can in a sticker bush. He raised the saddlebag into place behind the saddle, tying it on.

"You aren't as inexperienced as you think you are." Lexie sidled up to him, her big blues transfixing him.

"Hey, I watch Westerns. I've seen how it's done."

"Westerns, huh? Another thing we have in common." Her dimples bracketed her rosebud mouth as she grinned.

The effect was akin to a thrown grenade about to blow. Every instinct he had shouted at him to retreat, but he stayed where he was. "It looks like our lunch is secure."

"At least you know what's important."

"Always." And he did. It was her. If he let her be.

"Ready to mount up, partner?" She tipped her light

gray Stetson, a perfect contrast to her ebony hair and porcelain complexion. "I'll introduce you to Red."

"He's been eyeballing me like I'm going to be toast." His attention might be firmly on Lexie, but he hadn't missed the horse on the other side of Pogo, keeping careful watch. "He looks bigger up close."

"He's a sweetie, so don't worry. I've told him all about you." She dismissed his concern with a wave of her hand, ducking under her horse's lead rope. "Hey, good boy. This is Pierce."

"Hi, Red." He held out his hand for the horse to scent. "Here's hoping we're going to be friends."

"If you want to mount up, I'll untie him." She was all business, patting the horse's neck, knotting the reins and dropping them over the saddle horn. "Ready?"

"I'll go anywhere with you, pretty lady." He hoped the Western movie drawl would cover what he didn't want her to hear, what he couldn't give in to feeling. He tied the small duffel behind the saddle. With one foot in the stirrup, he swung up and over. The creak of leather, the shift of the horse adjusting to his weight, and the distance to the ground kept his attention off Lexie, but it didn't keep her out of his heart.

No, she walked away with it as she unhooked the tie. "I'm assuming you remember the basics."

"Tuck and roll," he quipped. He wasn't afraid of falling off the horse. He wasn't afraid of crashing and burning. He'd done it before. He faced greater problems in his workday. He had his armor up, his vulnerabilities protected, and his faith on. Surely God hadn't brought him here for heartache. This was a stolen moment out of his life, one of quality and substance, one he had to leave behind come Sunday morning. It wasn't as if he had a chance of winning Lexie's heart or, even more importantly, a chance of keeping it.

He did win her laughter as she shook her head, striding away from him. She untied Pogo and mounted up, efficient and practiced. She sat a saddle straight and relaxed, as if she had been born to it.

"Follow me, soldier," she winked, reined Pogo around and rode straight into the golden shafts of the morning light.

"Are you still back there?" she called over her shoulder, leaning forward in her saddle as Pogo climbed the rocky trail. A pleasant hour had passed, and Pierce hadn't fallen once. But she wanted to keep her eye on him anyway.

"Yep." His voice came from farther down the trail, around the wooded bend, out of sight.

That was it. Just "yep," and no elaboration. She eased Pogo to a stop and waited, twisting around for a better view. Red's hooves chinked on the rocky trail, growing closer. The leaves overhead whispered as the breeze lazed through them, sifting the light. The moment Pierce cornered the grove of aspen, the joy lifting through her doubled.

"Sorry, I saw a red-tailed hawk back there. I slowed the horse to take a look."

"There's a pair that nests somewhere around here. I've seen them a lot this summer. Maybe we'll see them hunting."

"Maybe." His smile could stop the earth from spinning. It sure made her world come to a standstill.

She pressed her heels gently against Pogo's sides and he moved forward, powering to the top of the hill.

Above the music of birdsong and rustling wild grasses and leaves rose the melody of running water. The trees gave way to a meadow bright with flowers, their round faces open toward the sun. Light glinted and seared off the crystal clear creek ribboning along its edge.

"Wow." He drew Red up alongside her. "This is the creek you waded in when you were young."

"Yes. And around that big boulder, where the aspens are? That's where it's deep enough to swim." She swept off her hat and fanned herself with it a few times. She was baking. The horses meandered through the field, trekking through sunflowers, purple coneflowers and crimson Indian paint. Deer tracks cut into the earth near the water's edge, and a few other tracks she knew all too well.

"Looks like we've had both cougar and bear here." She dismounted, reins in hand, and knelt to get a closer look.

Pierce joined her at the bank, his capable presence sending a shiver through her.

"It's fresh." He took off his glasses, carefully scanning the undergrowth of the tree line across the water. "Will the horses be safe?"

"We'll keep an eye on them to make sure. This is nothing unusual, although the bear might be interested in the saddlebag."

"I'll separate it from the horse, just in case." He wasn't the kind of guy who got ruffled easily, she thought, watching him as he untied his duffel. From the first moment she'd met him, she had liked the stalwart capability he radiated, but it wasn't superficial—just the tip of the iceberg.

"I learned that the hard way once." He'd pulled two

towels from his bag, slung them over his wide shoulder, before he came for her pack. "We were out tromping through our acreage with our dog. He's gone now. Spotty was kind of old, so he rolled up in our stuff to take a siesta. Hawk, Tim and I were up to our knees in the creek, watching the crawdads, and next thing we knew, there was a bear."

"Something tells me he was more interested in the dog than the food you'd brought?"

"So much for the bologna sandwiches. I was about eight, I guess. I threw a rock at the bear, hit him in the knee. He left the dog alone all right, but he came after me. I ran. Hawk ran. Tim ran. The dog ran. You never saw any kids in the history of the world sprint as fast as we did that day." Laughing, he hung the bags on a thick aspen branch. "That was the last time Spotty wanted to go to the creek with us. Tim had nightmares for months."

"You miss him a lot, don't you?"

"More than anything. We were tight." He didn't look at her. He concentrated on the scenery, the breathtaking peaks of the Rockies spearing up into the deep blue sky, the playful water beckoning him, and the memories he couldn't let himself forget. "We spent most of our time together. Losing him is something I'm never going to get over."

"Nor should you. He was your brother." She'd tossed aside her hat and sunglasses, too, standing near him with her cloth sneakers at the water's edge, her heart wide-open in understanding. He could feel the balm of it in his soul.

"He would have liked you." He swallowed hard, keeping his emotions down. "Of course, you're a Wyoming girl, so that might have something to do with it."

"Probably." Her hand, so small and soft, yet strong in a different way, found his. Her voice was sweet with understanding, hearing what he could not say. "I have developed a real fondness for Wyoming guys."

He heard what she could not say. His eyes burned and he didn't want her to see how deeply she had touched him. She was more than his heart, she was part of his soul, too. He laced his fingers through hers, holding on tight. "That water looks mighty cold. On three. Ready? One. Two—"

"Three," they said together, jumping into the water side by side, in perfect harmony.

Chapter Thirteen

"How's the cotton candy?" He leaned close as they maneuvered the small town's main street together, weaving around knots of people and arts and crafts booths.

"Perfect." Lexie held out the paper cone heaped with pink fluff for him to taste for himself.

The day had been unparalleled. After swimming, splashing and jumping off the boulder to Pierce's shouts of "banzai", and a lunch of Aunt Julia's remarkable barbecue beef sandwiches and a lot more swimming, they had ridden back to the ranch, watching wildlife along the way. They'd not only spotted the hawks circling gracefully overhead, hunting, but sighted both an elk and a moose.

After the barn work, Pierce had driven them into town, where they'd meandered through the arts and crafts booths on Second Street and the horse sale in the fire department's lot. After trolling the food booths, Pierce had bought them cheeseburgers, a huge tube of crinkle fries and icy milkshakes and they had sat on the schoolyard lawn to eat. She had laughed so much all day that her face hurt, as did a dozen muscles in her abdomen she didn't know she had.

"I'll be the judge of that." Pierce plucked a couple inches of pink fluff from the cotton cone and popped it in his mouth. "You're right. Perfect."

The way he looked into her eyes as he said that word made her feet miss the ground. She was aware of nearly stumbling and of the scuff of her sneaker against the pavement. Why did she get the feeling that he wasn't talking about the cotton candy any more than she had been? And worse, why was she so caught up in Pierce, that she wasn't watching where they were going?

"The fairgrounds is over this way." She nudged him to the right. "We don't want to miss the rodeo, right?"

"Right, seeing as that's the reason we came."

"Lexie!" A familiar voice cut through the din of the noisy street fair.

She whirled around, squinting into the shadows on the other side of the street. Seated in a booth of sparkling gold and silver, a blond-haired girl waved. Recognizing her old grade school friend, she brushed Pierce's arm to signal him. The casual touch between friends ought to have no effect on her, but it rattled through her like panic.

"A friend of yours?" He leaned closer than simple friendship would allow.

"Y-yes." The word caught in her throat. She was afraid of his closeness, but more afraid of him moving away. She was vaguely aware of crossing the street, of him protecting her from the small crowd as they headed to the booth.

"Lexie! I've been meaning to call you." Lu leaned over the counter, all smiles. "Who is this?"

"A friend of mine. Pierce, this is Lu. We've been friends since second grade." The panic stuttered through her, and when his steely arm brushed her shoulder, she didn't move away. Neither did he. "That's when Lu's family moved to Swinging Rope, and she sat next to me in the lunchroom."

"I obviously have excellent taste in friends," Lu quipped. "And so does Lexie. It's nice to meet you, Pierce."

"Likewise. You make this jewelry?"

"Are you kidding? I just work here. So, are you two heading over to the fairgrounds like everyone else? Do you see anything that catches your eye?"

Lexie groaned. She couldn't believe her ears. Oh, she knew *exactly* what Lu was thinking. "Pierce, don't pay any attention to her. Lu, I'll see you Wednesday evening."

"Now hold on." Easygoing, that was Pierce, one hand settling on the curve of her shoulder, pinning her gently in place. "I see something I like."

"You're big on jewelry, are you?" Her knees were trembly. The pressure of his hand on her shoulder felt like a branding iron. She wanted to bolt; she wanted to get closer.

"I'm a big fan of it." He lifted his hand from her shoulder, offering her blessed relief and disappointment all at once. Before she could take a breath, the pleasant weight of his entire arm settled over her shoulder, drawing her to him. He was sun-warmed granite as he held her close. "I want to see those blue beads."

The urge to bolt heightened, the only thing stronger was her wish to stay in the security of his embrace, pleasantly trapped by his warm strength.

"You have great taste." Lu was way too helpful, practically trilling as she turned to the numerous, breath taking displays. "These lapis beads match her eyes perfectly."

"That's the idea." He wasn't looking at Lu; his gaze never left hers. "Do you like them?"

"Are you kidding? That isn't the question you should be asking me." Of course she loved them. Anyone would. The trouble was, the impossible hope laying in wait within her was paying attention. It stirred, wanting to read something into this, that could only be a friendship gift. "You don't need to do this. It's too extravagant."

"I'll be the judge of that." His arm slipped from her shoulders to unhook the necklace, a richly gleaming strand of true blue. He placed it around her neck with a brush of his knuckles, his nearness making her dizzy as he leaned in to secure the clasp. His tenderness as he brushed a lock of hair from her face was unmistakable. The way he looked at her was agonizingly sweet.

Aunt Julie was right. The way he gazed at her made her feel beloved. The beads felt cool against her throat, but the man before her was pure tender warmth, his heart exposed, his love for her quiet and ocean-deep. He loved her as wholly as she loved him. Silent joy twinkled through her. All the sharp edges of her fears remained, but her singular love for him was far greater than any fear.

"Perfect." He breathed, stepped away, his hand cupping her shoulder and gently turning her toward a small mirror tacked on a two-by-four.

Perfect. There was that word again, and it had nothing to do with the exquisite necklace or the post earrings he held up for her to take. Or the matching bracelet he slid around her wrist.

"A little something to remember this day by." He explained as he handed over his credit card. "It's been a good day."

"Very good," she agreed, hearing what he didn't say. It had been perfection.

"Nearly the entire population of Swinging Rope is here," Lexie leaned closer, her breath warm on his ear, her hair silken wonder against his jaw. "The rodeo is a huge deal around here. Everyone comes in from out of town. Look, there's Uncle Bill and Aunt Julie."

He did his best to focus in the direction she was nodding, across the span of the dirt field, to the far end of the stands. Bill and Julie sat side by side, sharing comments on the event in the way established, married folk did. They made a nice couple. Everything about them shouted happy from the cozy way they snuggled shoulder to shoulder to the way she whispered something and they chuckled together. Anyone could see they shared the same sense of humor, the same values and dreams in life, and a day-by-day intimacy that love required.

Love didn't prosper on a long-distance basis. Not most love, anyway. He thought of his buddies whose marriages had fallen apart and his own experience with trying to make an engagement work while on nearly constant deployment. Total disaster.

"That's my cousin Sally sitting with them," Lexie was saying, "Two rows up and over. See the pink shirt? Merritt is another old friend of mine. We've been friends since we were in little tot Sunday school together."

"I bet you were a cute kid." It was easy to visualize the little girl she used to be with a pixie's face and black pig tails. "Your roots go deep in this town."

"They do. You know how it is. You have roots, too."

His guts seized up, making the cotton candy he'd just had curl in his stomach. He didn't have roots, not really, not anymore. He shifted away from her and although he had leaned back only a few inches, it may as well have been a mile.

"I suppose you hope to come back here after school," he said carefully, casually, telling himself that her answer didn't matter. He couldn't afford to let it matter.

"I can't say that I haven't thought about it, because I have. That's Ruby." She waved to a red-haired girl at the bottom of the grandstand wearing chaps and leading a horse. "Anyway, I've put it in prayer and I'm leaving it up to God. He will guide me where He wants me to go. I'm confident of it."

"But you're hoping that it's here." He couldn't let it go. Her life was already firmly grounded in the dozen friends who had called out or stopped her to chat throughout the evening. She had family here and her horse. He could see her coming back to this town after she finished her degree, setting out a shingle and building herself a nice little practice. She might have said she could be happy anywhere, but his gut told him here was where she might be happiest. "You have plenty of friends, but what about guys? Any old flames you want to point out?"

"Ha! I don't have any old flames." Amusement sparkled, changing her yet again into someone new, someone he couldn't live without. She was friend and confidante, both a safe harbor and a rocky shore. He wasn't safe with her.

"I don't believe it." He kept talking when he should have stayed silent. Stayed sitting when he should have walked away. "You must have broken more than a few hearts here."

"Not a single one. Believe me. I didn't have one date in high school, either here or in Great Falls. Moving my freshman year didn't help, but it wasn't the reason I was never asked out." She didn't look troubled by it, but he could see her shadows.

"Why not?" He had to know. He couldn't imagine any guy not wanting to love Lexie for the rest of his life. That's pretty much how he felt.

"It was all me. I give off a stay-away vibe."

"I've never noticed it."

"When we met, I was down and out. All my energy was going to my broken ankle and all that pain, so there wasn't any mental waves left over to give you the vibe." Twin dimples bracketed her cute grin, but the shadows, the hurt, remained. He could feel it as if it were his own.

That right there was another sign he'd let things go too far. Pull away now, man, he ordered himself, while you still can. But did he listen?

No. He foolishly caught her amazingly delicate hand in his, and it fit just right within his own. He twined their fingers together and held on to her. "What exactly is this vibe?"

"Inquiring minds want to know, is that it?" She avoided his gaze and his question, but he wouldn't let her avoid him. He tightened his fingers around hers, gently, soothingly, so she would know she was safe with him.

A roar from the crowd lifted through the stands, but it wasn't powerful enough to disturb the moment between them. Her hand in his felt small, and her fingers held on to his with silent need.

Like a key turning a lock, his armor went down and he sat defenseless beside her, his heart wide-open, his most vulnerable self undefended.

"I'm afraid to trust someone." Her confession was a whisper, but the weight of it rang in the caverns of his soul. "My dad and I were close. He loved horses, too. Remember how I told you he took me to get Pogo? We did nearly everything together. I was fourteen when he left. Without warning. Without a clue. I had choir practice after school, and I was waiting outside the back of the gym, waiting for him to come pick me up. I was angry at him for being late. I was the only kid there, waiting in the rain. He never came."

"Did you ever talk to him after that?"

"Not for a long time, and it devastated me. It was right before I graduated from high school. He said he had messed up and handled it the wrong way. Yeah, running out and leaving us without a single word was definitely the wrong way. I could never trust him again. We've made our peace, but I know who he is now. I'll never be able to see him the same way as I did when I was young and he was larger than life."

"So you're afraid that's how it's going to be. You will need someone and they'll leave you hanging?"

"Pretty much." She shrugged, her slim shoulder looked so frail to him; she was vulnerable, too, revealed. "I suppose it's basic psychology. I give guys the vibe so they stay away from me. So there's no risk at all of having to deal with trying to trust someone. Because deep down I don't think it's going to happen."

"Understandable." The crashing he heard was his

soul hitting bottom. She never would want a man like him, a man who couldn't be a rock for her, there whenever she needed him. He drew in a shaky breath, fighting to keep the pain from showing. A man had his pride.

Down on the floor, the calf tried to dodge the lasso, but it slipped tight around him and down he went, neatly into the soft dirt, hobbled and tied. The cowgirl's hands went up in the air, signaling she was done. Wild applause and deafening shouts of congratulations broke out as the announcer shouted the awesome time.

"Well, Ruby's won it for sure, so it's safe for me to leave." Lexie lifted a hand to stifle a yawn. "It's getting late."

"Especially if you have calves to feed come morning." Withdrawing his feelings and pulling on his armor, he stood and eased into the aisle. "Early to bed, early to rise."

"That's country life." Her smile was his dream as she made her way along the rail.

Every step he took down those bleachers was like a bayonet inching deeper into him. His armor was up, but that didn't help. It trapped the pain beneath the steel, and the wounds began to bleed. He felt every one of them as he joined her on the grass and they walked out of the stadium together. The noise from the calf-roping competition followed them like a spot of blue on a stormy day.

"Julie wanted to invite you to attend church with us tomorrow." She swished a lock of dark hair behind her ear. The rosy glow of sunset cast a soft, sepia light over her, like a blessing.

Everything within him longed for her, his friend, his dream. He squared his shoulders, determined to do the right thing for her. He would make this easy and keep friendship between them. "I'll think about it. I was going to get up early and drive to my parents' place."

"I'm sure your mom would love that." She shoved her hands into her pockets. "Julie will understand."

"I hope so." He kept pace with her, adjusting his long-legged stride to match hers. "That doesn't change anything between us, right?"

"Right." The necklace was warm against her skin, a reminder of the day and of this amazing time with him. Love brimmed over the rim of her heart, making the world twice as beautiful and three times more hopeful.

She had opened up to him tonight, and it felt as if a weight had been lifted. She had set her standards for a guy so high, hoping that would protect her from being hurt. But that wasn't the real issue. Life wasn't easy, and neither was love. She had thought that the trick would be in finding a good, noble man who would love her wholly; but she had to open her heart and do the same. Love was a verb, in doing and in feeling.

She'd been cautiously looking for the right guy to date for most of her adult life. Forgoing innocent outings in high school for ice cream or a movie and bypassing lots of nice guys at college believing that if only she found the best guy, the flawless, most loyal, most trustworthy guy ever, she would never get hurt. That she could be loved without fear of loss or abandonment or betrayal.

Talk about being naive. That had been all about protecting her heart, which was impossible. She was walking beside the most trustworthy guy ever, a man she thought was the true definition of the word, and her heart broke ever more, this time in deeper fractures that ripped all the way to her soul. Loving hurt, in a sweet but painful way. Real love was all risk and all heartbreak and no security. She could see that now. She'd been trying to keep herself safe, but in doing so, she had closed up her heart. Loving was a two-way street. She had to risk, too, and open her heart completely.

Fear tripped into her, trembling through her veins. Her instinct was to stay safely in her shell. To keep walking alongside the road where parked cars lined up like one long freight train and talk of easy things, like how cute the little kids' calf-roping event had been or her friend Ruby's amazing rope time.

But she wanted more. As her sneakers crunched in the gravel alongside the road, she glanced at Pierce through her lashes. Those unnamed wishes within her grew like seedlings to sun. She dared to imagine life with this man, of sharing his laughter and his heartaches, of having him at her side to share hers.

He must have been watching her, too, because his smile grew to meet hers, and love kicked through her. They walked in time, their shoes crunching in the roadside gravel in unity. Taking the biggest risk of her life, she let her hand brush Pierce's with a silent question.

In answer, his fingers twined with hers, linking them as they walked, much more than friends as they strolled toward the brilliant sunset. His truck loomed up out of the eye-blinding light, a giant shadow she was hardly aware of. All she could think of, all she could feel was the contact of his palm to hers and the thrill of the silence between them, a silence filled with language.

Love. It was the way he opened the passenger door for her, a gentleman to the core, the way he held her hand as if loath to break the contact and connection between them. Her spine dug into the truck's side panel as she lingered, hating to let him go, too. Their hearts beat together as he brushed his knuckles down the angle of her cheek, hesitating at the corner of her mouth.

His eyes were luminous as they searched hers, seeing more than anyone ever had. She kept her heart open, more vulnerable than she had ever been, changed by her love for this man. Her fear faded as his thumb traced her bottom lip with a feather-soft question.

One her heart answered. He must have heard because he leaned closer and closer still, in no hurry, savoring the moment as his mouth hovered over hers. The sunset glow seemed to blind her as his lips found hers, the sweetest warm brush of a kiss, and then another so tender, tears burned behind her eyes. She wanted forever with this man.

She clung to his shirt, awed by his love, and when he stepped away, the intimacy did not stop. His gaze fastened on hers with a greater impact than any touch, any word, any vow. In that silence, she felt him touch her heart as easily as the last of the sunlight touched her face. Love infused the air, unmistakable and true, an impossible prayer answered.

She thought she saw a great sadness shadowed in his eyes the instant before he tore away, but how could that be? Maybe it was only the shadows from the setting sun, still sinking behind the mountains, its slow nightly dance winding down.

As they drove home in silence, she couldn't be sure.

Those kisses. It was the only thing Pierce could think about as he navigated the gravel driveway that snaked along the wood and wire fence posts to the Evanses's ranch house. Twilight had faded, night had come, and stars cluttered the inky sky like dreams he could not give in to. Those kisses shouldn't have happened. Nope, not at all.

Where had his self-discipline gone? Where was his resolve? He knew who he was, but when he was with Lexie, he wanted to be someone else. A man who could be all that she needed, all she deserved.

But he'd signed a contract promising to serve his country for another four years. He was in, all in, and there was no going back. It was nonnegotiable. And even if it were, being a Ranger was integral to him. It was everything he believed in. How could he turn his back on his calling? Worse, how could he turn his back on Lexie?

No, he couldn't do that. Their kiss had changed him. He'd been living on cloud nine, carried away by the happiness of the day and the dream of her. Walking away from the grandstand, he never should have taken her hand. He never should have given in to the swell of love and devotion and, worse, he absolutely never should have kissed her. Because in that kiss was the hope for more than he could possibly deliver. His life wasn't his own. That was the sacrifice of service. Any minute his phone could ring and he would be back on base, reporting for duty regardless of what he wanted or what Lexie needed.

She deserved to have everything. His love for her doubled when he looked at her. He killed the headlights and pulled to a stop in the driveway. As he cut the engine, he popped open the door so she couldn't turn to him and draw him in with her soulful blue eyes. His feet hit the ground, and as he circled around the truck, he gathered up his resolve. He could feel the weight of her gaze on him. It was like a tractor beam to his heart. So what if he wanted to kiss her? He wasn't going to do it. He was going to do the right thing, say good-night and goodbye to her because there was no way on God's green earth this could work.

It was time to get real. He whipped open her door, drew himself up to full height and faced the fire.

"Thanks for such a wonderful day." Her hand caught his and she slid lightly to the ground. There was enough illumination from the floodlight above the garage and the star shine to see her joy. She glowed from the inside out, radiating a beauty that hooked him harder and at a deeper level.

How was he ever going to be able to let her go? He shut the door with force, and it ricocheted through the still yard like a gunshot.

"I had a good time, too." It was only the truth; it was less than he wanted to say. "It more than makes up for the afternoon of skiing you cost me."

"That's right. I never made that up to you." She fell in line with him as they headed up the walk to the front door. "Maybe you will have some leave coming next winter and you can visit. I'll treat you to a day of skiing."

"That's an offer I can't refuse—" He paused in mid-stride. "But I have to."

"You'll probably be on a tour of duty." She stopped beside him with the sweep of dark lawn and star-studded sky framing her. "Right, I understand. Then I'll take a rain check. No biggie."

Something had changed for her, too. She sparkled like stardust, quietly, lovely, but it was there all the same. Their kiss stood between them, and he couldn't take it back. He wished more than anything that kiss hadn't happened. She felt this, too, this closeness he could no longer deny. He had to fight it. He had to do the right thing. He took her hand in his.

Best to nip this in the bud before she got hurt, because he was already there. The idea of never seeing her again was like the stars going out and the sun never rising again. He was a tough man and he'd faced a lot of difficulties, but nothing could top having to break this off.

"No." He hardened his heart, gathering up his armor. "I can't do a rain check, either."

"You don't plan on coming back to the States for a long time?" Confusion etched her lovely face. "You never said if you were going overseas. It must be for a very long deployment."

"No, I'm talking about us, Lexie. Our friendship." There, he'd gotten that much out without stuttering or changing his mind. So far, so good. He straightened his spine, ready to face the rest of what had to be done. "Don't get me wrong. This time getting to know you has meant everything to me—"

"To me, too." Her hand squeezed his gently, an invitation of the heart.

One he had to gently decline. It was going to kill him.

"I'm so glad you could come by." Affection warmed her words, made the evening beyond compare. "I know you're leaving in the morning, but we can keep in touch with e-mail. Maybe a phone call now and then."

"I don't know about that." Careful, he let go of her hand, let go of her. "Tonight with you, kissing you, it's not what I signed on for."

He saw the exact moment when his words dawned. The star shine faded from her like the last light going out. He stood in darkness.

Chapter Fourteen

His words echoed within her, and like a quick, breaking blow she felt nothing but shock. Had she been wrong? No, she'd felt his love in their kiss. She'd witnessed it in his touch and in his tenderness. He loved her, but he didn't want her?

"I've told you that love is one battlefield I intend to stay off." He seemed like part of the night, like a lost soul at world's end. "I'm sorry. I didn't mean for things to get this far."

"Neither did I." She held herself very still. Maybe if she didn't breathe and if her heart didn't beat, then the shock wouldn't wear off. Maybe she could stay in this numb place, still reeling from his rejection and never feel the crash. "It snuck up on us."

"Yes. I sure didn't plan this. I came to see you because staying away was torture. I thought I could see you, convince myself I was better off without you. I could go on with my life, leave you to go on with yours." His words rang harsh, but his tone resonated with kindness.

That kindness lured her, creeping through her numbness, forcing her to feel.

"You came to get rid of me?" She knew that wasn't what he was saying, but it's what she chose to see. It was easier to see one side instead of both. Her heart would break less if she thought he was cruel rather than knowing it was torturing him, too. No longer numb, pain sideswiped her, knocking her as if to her knees. Air caught like a sob in her throat. It all made sense. The long silences. "You stopped writing to me. I should have known."

She should have protected her heart better. She should have listened to that part of her warning her to be wary, to protect herself, to stay distant instead of getting close. *That's* what she should have done. Instead, she had fallen for his tender charm and caring gestures, for the sense of rightness that formed between them whenever they were together. She had fallen for the wrong man, when she had known it all along.

Tears burned behind her eyes and she blinked hard, defying them. Anger simmered in her midsection, anger at him for making her love him endlessly, beyond all reason.

"I'm no good at this, Lexie." He sounded hollowed out, as if he were hurting, too. "I told you that. I can't deny that I was hoping maybe, just maybe. But I'm a realist. I don't have time for anything else. This is never going to work."

"Sure, if you say so." She retreated backward down the walk, knowing the house was behind her somewhere.

Hold it together, Lexie, she told herself, swallowing against the stubborn tears balled in her throat. It was only five steps up to the porch. Five steps across the porch to the front door. Ten steps. That's how long she had to keep the tears out of her eyes and her soul from shattering. Once she let the door click shut and she was safely by herself, she could let the tears come. She could let the devastation fall. But not one moment before.

She fisted her hands, hardly hearing what Pierce was saying. Something about being gone, how it hadn't worked before.

"I can't see it working out." He came toward her, moving out of the darkness until he was glossed by star shine, standing tough and self-contained, so strong he didn't need anyone. Especially her. He kept talking, as if trying to make her see. "We could probably make it work for a while, but you've got your program to finish and I've got deployments. We're going to spend more time apart than together. You'll start dreading a knock at the door or the phone ringing because it could bring bad news."

"I know this." The anger inside of her was building, which wasn't really anger at all. She took another step back. Eight left to go. A sob caught in her windpipe. "These are just excuses, Pierce. I know, because I went through them, too. I've gone through every reason why we should stay apart. Every single one, so I don't need to hear them from you."

"I don't want it to be like this. I don't want to hurt you." His baritone dipped with unmistakable affection. "I think it's best for us to end this now, before we both get our hearts broken."

"Speak for yourself," she croaked out the words, fighting down another sob. "It's too late."

"No, it can't be. You can't fall for a man like me." He sounded certain, as if that were an established fact.

"What kind of man would that be? The kind who carries an injured woman to safety? Who brings her lunch and text messages during Bach? Who shares his secrets with her? Who makes her feel safe enough to push past every fear and fall in love with him?"

"What did you say?" He shook his head. Something must be wrong with his hearing. He wasn't getting something right. "You've fallen in love with me?"

"Not anymore." Her chin shot up. In the shadows of the porch, she was darkness itself, but her voice revealed everything.

He heard the held back tears and the stifled sob. He felt the edges of her pain. Head hung, he chastised himself. He never would have said it that way if he'd thought she loved him. She was in *love* with him? He'd thought he was alone with that particular emotion. That he had been the one falling for her, and it was his heart, his soul, on the line.

But he'd been wrong. "Lexie, I'm sorry—"

"Sure you are." She sounded angry, but he knew she was hurting. He could feel the twist of it in his chest and the bleak darkness of what was now lost. Her chin shot up. "You have all these reasons, and I know they're good ones. I have them, too. All I know is that I made a mistake. You've said what you need to, so just go."

"No, I can't leave you like this."

"I'll be fine. I need you to leave." She retreated into the shadows. There was the faint rattle of a doorknob, and the night stretched between them, wide and dark and impossible to breach. She had withdrawn her heart, leaving him alone in the shadows. Hinges whispered, her sneakers padded on the hardwood floor.

This was his last look at her, his last chance to say the right thing, but he didn't know what it was. Even if she was in love with him, how could it be enough? She had all this, roots, family and friends and goals to pursue. She could have any man she wanted, she was fantastic, gorgeous and deeply good. She deserved to have a man there for her. He wanted with all of his soul to be that man.

As he backtracked to the truck, his loss hit deep. He was too nail-tough for tears, but they burned in the back of his eyes anyhow. He wrestled them down, stilling his feelings, putting back on his armor. The night wind puffed hot against his face as he opened the truck door. Her scent of lilacs and summer sunshine and sweetness tormented him as he settled behind the wheel.

Every bit of him longed for her, to have her beside him on that seat. He ached for the sanctuary he'd found in her arms. He yearned for her brightness with all the scarred places in his soul. His love for her beat through him as infinite as the sky, as endless as eternity and he could not make himself turn the key in the ignition. Somehow he had to find his common sense and the strength to drive away.

He didn't have it. He sat there, hand on the steering wheel, his forehead on his hand, his pulse hitting like a mace against his ribs, the night sounds surrounding him. Somewhere a coyote howled. A barn owl swooped low over the truck's windshield, dark wings spread wide.

I'm a stubborn man, Lord. Please help me do this one thing. Please give me the strength to walk away. He didn't feel an answer on the breeze ruffling through his hair, but he did look into the future. What did he see? A happy courtship, a nice wedding with Lexie, beautiful in a white floor-length gown, maybe even a year or two of happiness. But what then?

The image of months on end of e-mails and an occasional phone call, that's what made him turn the key. The engine roared to life, blasting unnaturally loud in the still night. But there would come a time, he knew, when that contact wasn't enough. She would need him and he would be half a world away, and then what? Her disappointment would add up, her hurt would mount, and she would fall out of love with him.

That destroyed him down to the quick. He backed around and nosed the truck down the driveway, refusing to let his gaze drift to the rearview mirror. He needed to see her, he wanted it with his entire being, but he had to keep going. Because if he caught sight of her, just one tiny glance, he couldn't do it. He couldn't walk away and he would doom them to disaster, an untenable situation.

He wheeled the truck around the first bend, the headlights slicing shafts of light along the fence-lined road. Every inch, every foot, every yard he drove took him farther away from her. He wrestled with an unnamed pain. The tangle of emotion in his chest, knotted up all this time, unraveled strand by strand. He needed her. He loved her. His devotion to her was strong enough to withstand everything.

If only that was enough. He hated the burning lump in his throat and the hurt hammering through him. If pain was weakness leaving the body, then he was surely purging an entire reserve of it tonight. Nothing in his life had hurt so much. Not shrapnel wounds, not a bullet wound, not one single experience in Ranger school when he'd gone without sleep, food, rest or comfort of any kind, and not even losing Tim. Nothing—not one thing—had prepared him for the agony cutting through his soul.

He'd lost her. Forever. He was supposed to have been

protecting himself from this kind of pain, and yet he'd walked right into an ambush. He'd never seen it coming, this love for her that would not end.

Lights swept around the next bend and into his eyes. He slowed to a crawl and wheeled onto as much of the shoulder as he could drive on, and the other vehicle did the same. He wasn't surprised to see the oncoming white truck stop next to him.

He stopped, too. The dashboard lights were enough to see Bill and Julie.

"Hope you enjoyed the rodeo," Bill called out. "Noticed you and Lexie left early."

"She needed to get home because of the calves." Their conversation in town seemed a millennium ago.

"Yep, four-thirty in the morning comes around awfully fast," Bill agreed, as Julie talked right over him.

"You're coming to Sunday service with us?"

"Sorry, ma'am. I'm driving up to attend church with my folks." He did his best to focus, but he was too torn up. All he wanted was to get as far away as possible. The wound ran deep, as if mortal. "Good night, and thanks again for your hospitality."

"It was our pleasure." Julie beamed. Anyone could see she thought he and Lexie were a couple.

What he would give if they could be. Armor up, he did his best to deflect his feelings. It wasn't working. There was a hollow in him where her love used to be.

"Hope to see you again soon, son." Bill lifted a hand in farewell, put the truck in gear and rolled forward into the night.

Alone, Pierce waited on the side of the road, breathing deep, drawing the fresh country air in, willing the pain out. He could stay in the Army, he thought, but change jobs. He could find something that would keep him mostly on his base, it wouldn't satisfy him quite the same way, but at least he could have a chance with her.

He leaned his forehead on the steering wheel, confused, coming apart, and yet knowing his job was more than just a job. Did he go back to her and give up his calling in order to keep her? Or did he continue driving alone in the dark?

A little help, Lord, please. He opened his heart to heaven, craving God's grace, but he was in too much turmoil to feel an answer. He only knew that he loved her.

Well, it wasn't as if he could sit here all night. He lifted his head, feeling wrung out and in pieces. He eased his foot off the brake, letting the truck roll forward. Something flashed in his peripheral vision. The taillights from Bill's truck glancing across the side view mirror. But it wasn't the light that caught his attention.

He turned in the seat, against the restraint of the belt, to get a look at the shadows in the mirror. The shadow of a young woman slumped in a chair, with her face in her hands, a look of utter heartbreak. He had a perfect view of the Evanses's back patio.

Lexie. Crying. He slammed on the brake, feeling his armor tumble down. He stared at her image, one of abject pain. She hurt that much? He thought back to her voice, rising out of the shadows, choked with a stifled sob. He'd known he was hurting her, but surely she didn't feel so deeply about him. Surely she didn't share this soul-binding, life-changing all-out love?

He opened the truck door and dropped to the road. He paced to the shoulder, searching through the night shadows for her. When he saw her again, his heart became whole. He hopped the fence and humped through the field, seed-topped grasses and wildflowers brushing him as he went. Horses in the pasture looked up, tracking him curiously as he vaulted the fence on the other side, landing behind Julie's vegetable garden. He trailed the knee-high row of corn to the garden's edge.

There she was, still as stone, except for the shake of her shoulders. He'd done this to her. He'd broken her heart. He could feel the waves of pain reeling into him. The strength ebbed from his knees. Vulnerable, he stumbled in the darkness, no longer lost, seeing only her. Just her and her love for him, strong enough to endure distance and time. He could see that now.

His dear, precious Lexie. He didn't remember crossing the lawn or the moment his shoe hit the smooth concrete surface. His heart pulled him to her like a safety net, reeling him in. She sensed him, lifting her face from her hands, already stiffening up and swiping away her tears.

"Lexie." He was on his knees, helping her wipe away those tears. Tenderness surged through him like a tidal wave, drowning out every doubt, every worry and every fear. For the first time in what felt like forever, he was in sync with the world, as if he was exactly where he was meant to be. He knew now that he belonged with her. His purpose in life, beyond duty, was to love her.

"Wh-what are you doing here?" She went to push him away, to protect herself, but he didn't let her. He kept drying her tears, seeing the hurt he'd caused and hating himself for it. He would die before he would do it again.

"I came back." He brushed the last tear from her cheek. "I didn't realize how you felt. That you felt this much."

"Not anymore I don't." At least, that's the way she wanted it. She wanted to be able to turn off her heart, switch off her love for him and tell him she didn't need him. "You can go back to town guilt-free."

"I'm not here out of guilt." He caught her hands with his and held them captive, gently but firmly. Her tears were wet on his warm fingers. "I'm not going anywhere, sunshine. Not until you answer my question."

"You haven't asked any questions." Having him see her like this was torture. He'd seen her crying, he'd heard her sobbing and now he knew how much she'd loved him. "I know you said we were only going to be friends. I get that. You should leave."

"When I've only just got here?" He pressed a kiss to the back of her hand. "You can stop trying to push me away. I'm not going anywhere."

"Yes, you are. You're going to you see your parents in the morning." She pulled her hands from his grip. Every fiber of her being warned her to push him away and to keep pushing him. She was hurting and his presence here was sheer anguish.

"Change of plans." He leaned closer. His hands came up to cradle her chin, so lovingly he was in danger of capturing her heart again. "I'm going to spend my leave right here with you."

"With me?" She blinked furiously against the searing tears filling her eyes. "What about your folks?"

"They'll understand."

"What about Alaska?"

"Cancelled."

She didn't believe this. Her heart couldn't take it. "But you said this isn't what you signed on for. You said—"

"Forget what I said. Everything is different now." His thumb traced gentle circles on her bottom lip, reminding them both of their beautiful kisses. "I realized something. I don't want this to end. I'm in love with you. Flat out, all the way, point of no return in love."

"You are?" Those pesky tears were falling against her will.

"I am." His confirmation rang with whole truth and utter sincerity. "And if you feel the same way about me…?"

He let the question dangle, as if waiting for her answer. Trembling, she opened her heart the rest of the way, leaned her forehead on his wide, steely shoulder and let the tears fall. "Yes," she said into his shirt. "I love you too much. This is scaring me and h-hurting."

"For me, too." His hand settled on the back of her neck, cupping her lightly, all solid comfort. She could feel the reliable thump of his heart and, in the silence, his pledge. "It's going to be all right, sunshine, as long as you agree to one thing. Will you marry me?"

She straightened to look at him, joy leaking into her tears. "You want me to marry you?"

"That's why I'm asking."

Hope stirred in her heart, now healed and whole. She could see their future. A wedding with butter-yellow roses and a long white gown, a little house near his air base, spending every treasured moment they could together, the years going by bringing a baby or two and more joy than she could hold.

"There are a hundred reasons why I could say no," she told him, "but only one reason to say yes. I love you. I want to spend my life being loved by you."

"That's the plan, sunshine." He kissed her with exquisite tenderness, leaving no doubt that he was the one. The man she could trust above all others to love her for keeps.

Epilogue

Two years, five months later.

"**B**anzai!" A man's shout rang behind her on the mountainside.

At the top of the run, Lexie Granger had just enough time to glance over her shoulder. A tall, muscled guy in black launched off the lift, dug in with his poles and flew toward her in a blur.

Yeah, that was just what she expected of her husband, back from a thirteen-month tour of duty, glad to be hitting the slopes.

"I'll see you at the bottom, handsome!" she called out. The only sign that he heard her was the flash of his smile and a quick salute. She watched him speed away, taking her heart with him as he always did.

"Banzai!" A second man shot off the lift, flying down the slope in a streak of red.

"Those two." Lexie shook her head and adjusted her goggles.

"I know." September joined her, a friend she'd made

at Pogo's riding stable and Hawk's wife. "I don't know exactly what is wrong with those two, but I like it."

"Me, too."

The Washington State sky was a soft winter blue, the perfect backdrop as she pushed off, digging in with her poles to join her husband racing down the slope. The snow was fast, the air was fresh and after a long week of managing her thriving practice, nothing could be better than stealing away on a Friday afternoon to ski with her husband and their friends.

He had been back on U.S. soil for eight days now, and after two years of marriage, they had survived their first long deployment just fine. Phone calls and e-mails weren't the same as personal contact, but they had both tried hard to keep their love and relationship thriving.

As she rounded a curve, she caught sight of a black blur far down the run. Her soul brightened as it always did with love for her husband, for the man who had kept all his vows to her. He was faithful and tender and kind, and every day that passed she felt more treasured by him. Life was blissful, and their love perfection.

As he waited for her at the bottom of the run, she couldn't get down the rest of the slope fast enough to his waiting arms. Once she was enfolded against his steely chest, safe and protected in his embrace, she held him tight, brimming with bliss.

"I'm glad to be with you again," Pierce whispered, low so that only she could hear. "I love you, sunshine."

His words tinkled against her ear and she shivered, twinkling like starlight from the inside out. "I love you, Banzai Boy."

"Lucky me." His gaze searched hers, drawing out the moment, deepening their closeness.

They didn't need to speak for her to know what he was thinking. This morning lazing in front of the fire sipping tea and sharing the morning paper, talk had drifted to their future. To his decision to accept a promotion, which would largely take him out of the field. To the house that was for sale not far from Pogo's boarding stable. To planning for a baby sometime in the near future.

"No, lucky me," she corrected. Although luck had nothing to do with it. She paused to give thanks to God for His leading. She had no doubt that the Lord had brought her here, to the shelter of Pierce's arms, and their deep, enduring love that was the greatest blessing of all.

"How about another shot at that run?" Pierce's challenge made them both smile.

"I would love nothing more." Yes, she thought, it was going to be another wonderful day with the man she loved.

They took off together, side by side and heart to heart, graced by sunlight.

* * * * *

Don't miss Jillian Hart's
next Inspirational romance,
BLIND DATE BRIDE
From Love Inspired, available May 2009

Dear Reader,

You may remember Kelly's roommate Lexie from *A Soldier for Christmas*. I hope you do. When I was writing that book, the practical, interesting Lexie caught my attention. I wondered what her story was. Would she ever find a totally trustworthy man, like she was looking for? Why was she so distrustful in the first place? And because she gave Mitch, the hero in *A Soldier for Christmas,* a rare two thumbs up, I wondered if she might find a soldier of her own one day.

When I met Pierce Granger, I knew he was the man for Lexie. Stalwart, faithful, and a deeply committed Army Ranger. I could see him falling in love with her forever. But time had passed while I was writing the rest of the McKaslin Clan series, and Lexie had a few changes in her story. She was now in graduate school and coming off a painful breakup. She had trusted someone enough to open her heart, and she had been hurt. I wondered if she would keep Pierce at a safe distance forever and how she would find the strength to risk love another time. I hope you enjoyed watching God lead Lexie and Pierce to true love and their happily-ever-after.

Thank you so much for choosing *A Soldier for Keeps*.

Wishing you the best of blessings,

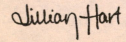

QUESTIONS FOR DISCUSSION

1. At the beginning of the story, how would you describe Lexie's character? What are her weaknesses and her strengths? How has her past influenced who she is?

2. When Lexie first sees Pierce, she doesn't have the best first impression of him. How does that change when he finds her injured on the slope? What character traits does she see in Pierce?

3. How does Lexie's decision to stay friends change throughout the story? Why does it change?

4. Why does Pierce open up to Lexie and tell her of his brother's loss? Why is this significant to him? How does it change his feelings toward her?

5. How does Pierce's story of his brother's loss change Lexie's view of him?

6. Lexie is struggling with abandonment and trust issues. How does God lead her through her fears? Have you ever struggled with similar issues?

7. Pierce thinks he's smart to be friends and nothing more with Lexie. He believes that it's better to remember how much love can hurt and stay away from it. Why does he think this? What are the signs through the story that his beliefs are changing?

8. Do you think Pierce's decision to stay in the Army is right or wrong? How is God's leading evident?

9. What role does Pierce's family play in the story?

10. When Lexie sits with Giselle waiting for news of Pierce, what does she learn? How does this affect the story?

11. What do you think are the important themes?

12. What makes Lexie realize she is totally and completely in love with Pierce?

13. How would you describe Lexie's faith? Pierce's faith? How are each strengthened through the story?

14. Why does Pierce finally believe that Lexie loves him enough to make a marriage work?

15. How do you know Pierce and Lexie will have a happy life together?

*Turn the page for a sneak preview of
bestselling author Jillian Hart's novella
"Finally a Family"*

*One of two heartwarming stories
celebrating motherhood in
IN A MOTHER'S ARMS*

*On sale April 2009, only from
Steeple Hill Love Inspired Historical.*

Chapter One

Montana Territory, 1884

Molly McKaslin sat in her rocking chair in her cozy little shanty with her favorite book in hand. The lush new-spring-green of the Montana prairie spread out before her like a painting, framed by the wooden window. The blue sky was without a single cloud to mar it. Lemony sunshine spilled over the land and across the open window's sill. The door was wedged open, letting the outside noises in—the snap of laundry on the clothesline and the chomping crunch of an animal grazing. My, it sounded terribly close.

The peaceful afternoon quiet shattered with a crash. She leaped to her feet to see her good—and only—china vase splintered on the newly washed wood floor. She stared in shock at the culprit standing at her other window. A golden cow with a white blaze down her face poked her head farther across the sill. The bovine gave a woeful moo. One look told her this was the only animal in the yard.

"And just what are you doing out on your own?" She set her book aside.

The cow lowed again. She was a small heifer, still probably more baby than adult. The cow lunged against the sill, straining toward the cookie racks on the table.

"At least I know how to catch you." She grabbed a cookie off the rack and the heifer's eyes widened. "I don't recognize you, so I don't think you belong here."

Molly skirted around the mess on the floor and headed toward the door. This was the consequence of agreeing to live in the country, when she had vowed never to do so again. But her path had led her to this opportunity, living on her cousin's land and helping the family. God had quite a sense of humor, indeed.

Before she could take two steps into the soft, lush grass surrounding her shanty, the cow came running, head down, big brown eyes fastened on the cookie. The ground shook.

Uh-oh. Molly's heart skipped two beats.

"No, Sukie, no!" High, girlish voices carried on the wind.

Molly briefly caught sight of two identical school-aged girls racing down the long dirt road. The animal was too single-minded to respond. She pounded the final few yards, her gaze fixed on the cookie.

"Stop, Sukie. Whoa." Molly kept her voice low and kindly firm. She knew cows responded to kindness better than to anything else. She also knew they were not good at stopping, so she dropped the cookie on the ground and neatly stepped out of the way. The cow skidded well past the cookie and the place where Molly had been standing.

"It's right here." She showed the cow where the

oatmeal treat was resting in the clean grass. While the animal backed up and nipped up the goody, Molly grabbed the cow's rope halter.

"Good. She didn't stomp you into bits." One of the girls said in serious relief. "She ran me over real good just last week."

"We thought you were a goner," the second girl said. "She's real nice, but she doesn't see very well."

"She sees well enough to have found me." Molly studied the girls. They both had identical black braids and golden-hazel eyes and fine-boned porcelain faces. One twin wore a green calico dress with matching sunbonnet, while the other wore blue. She recognized the girls from church and around town. "Aren't you the doctor's children?"

"Yep, that's us." The first girl offered a beaming, dimpled smile. "I'm Penelope and that's Prudence. We're real glad you found Sukie."

"We wouldn't want a cougar to get her."

"Or a bear."

What adorable children. A faint scattering of freckles dappled across their sun-kissed noses, and there was glint of trouble in their eyes as the twins looked at one another. The place in her soul thirsty for a child of her own ached painfully. She felt hollow and empty, as if her body would always remember carrying the baby she had lost. For one moment it was as if the wind died and the earth vanished.

"Hey, what is she eating?" One of the girls tumbled forward. "It smells like a cookie. You are a bad girl, Sukie."

"Did she walk into your house and eat off the counter?" Penelope wanted to know.

The grass crinkled beneath her feet as the cow tugged her toward the girls. "No, she went through the window."

Penelope went up on tiptoe. "I see them. They look real good."

Molly gazed down at their sweet and innocent faces. She wasn't fooled. Then again, she was a soft touch. "I'll see what I can do."

She headed back inside. "Do you girls need help getting the cow home?"

"No. She's real tame." Penelope and the cow trailed after her, hesitating outside the door. "We can lead her anywhere."

"Yeah, she only runs off when she's looking for us."

"Thank you so much, Mrs.—" Penelope took the napkin-wrapped stack of cookies. "We don't know your name."

"This is the McKaslin ranch," Prudence said thoughtfully. "But I know you're not Mrs. McKaslin."

"I'm the cousin. I moved here this last winter. You can call me Molly."

Penelope gave her twin a cookie. Beneath the brim of her sunbonnet, her face crinkled with serious thought. "You don't know our pa yet?"

"No, I only know Dr. Frost by reputation. I hear he's a fine doctor." That was all she knew. Of course she had seen his fancy black buggy speeding down the country roads at all hours. Sometimes she caught a brief sight of the man driving as the horse-drawn vehicle passed— an impression of a black Stetson, a strong granite profile and impressively wide shoulders.

Although she was on her own and free to marry, she paid little heed to eligible men. All she knew of Dr. Sam

Frost was that he was a widower and a father and a faithful man, for he often appeared very serious in church. She reached through the open door to where her coats hung on wall pegs and worked the sash off her winter wool.

Prudence smiled. "Our pa's real nice and you make good cookies."

"And you're real pretty." Penelope was so excited she didn't notice Sukie stealing her cookie. "Do you like Pa?"

"I don't know the man, so I can't like him. I suppose I can't dislike him, either." She bent to secure the sash around Sukie's halter. "Let me walk you girls across the road."

"You ought to come home with us." Penelope grinned. "Then you can meet Pa."

"Do you want to get married?" Penelope's feet were planted.

So were Prudence's. "Yes! You could marry Pa. Do you want to?"

"M-marry your pa?" Shock splashed over her like icy water.

"Sure. You could be our ma."

"And then Pa wouldn't be so lonely anymore."

Molly blinked. The words were starting to sink in. The poor girls, wishing so much for a mother that they would take any stranger who was kind to them. "No, I certainly cannot marry a perfect stranger, but thank you for asking. I would take you two in a heartbeat."

"You would?" Penelope looked surprised. "Really?"

"We're an awful lot of trouble. Our housekeeper said that three times today since church."

"Does your pa know you propose on his behalf?"

"Now he does." A deep baritone answered. Dr. Frost marched into sight, rounding the corner of the shanty. His hat brim shaded his face, casting shadows across his chiseled features, giving him an even more imposing appearance. "Girls! Home! Not another word."

"But we had to save Sukie."

"She could have been eaten by a wolf."

Molly watched the good doctor's mouth twitch. She couldn't be sure, but a flash of humor could have twinkled in the depths of his eyes.

"You must be the cousin." He swept off his hat. The twinkle faded from his eyes and the hint of a grin from his lips. It was clear that while his daughters amused him, she did not. "I had no idea you would be so young."

"And pretty," Penelope, obviously the troublemaker, added mischievously.

Molly's face heated. The poor girl must need glasses. Although Molly was still young, time and sadness had made its mark on her. The imposing man had turned into granite as he faced her. Of course he had overheard his daughters' proposal, so that might explain it.

She smiled and took a step away from him. "Dr. Frost, I'm glad you found your daughters. I was about ready to bring them back to you."

"I'll save you the trouble." He didn't look happy. "Girls, take that cow home. I need to stay and apologize to Miss McKaslin."

She was a "Mrs." but she didn't correct him. She had put away her black dresses and her grief. Her marriage had mostly been a long string of broken dreams. She did better when she didn't remember. "Please don't be too hard on the girls on my behalf. Sukie's arrival livened up my day."

"At least there was no harm done." He winced. "There was harm? What happened?"

"I didn't say a word."

"No, but I could see it on your face."

Had he been watching her so closely? Or had she been so unguarded? Perhaps it was his closeness. She could see bronze flecks in his gold eyes, and smell the scents of soap and spring clinging to his shirt. A spark of awareness snapped within her like a candle newly lit. "It was a vase. Sukie knocked it off my windowsill when she tried to eat the flowers, but it was an accident."

"The girls should take better care of their pet." He drew his broad shoulders into an unyielding line. He turned to check on the twins, who were progressing down the road. The wind ruffled his dark hair. He seemed distant. Lost. "How much was the vase worth?"

How did she tell him it was without price? Perhaps it would be best not to open that door to her heart. "It was simply a vase."

"No, it was more." He stared at his hat clutched in both hands. "Was it a gift?"

"No, it was my mother's."

"And is she gone?"

"Yes."

"Then I cannot pay you its true value. I'm sorry." His gaze met hers with startling intimacy. Perhaps a door was open to his heart, as well, because sadness tilted his eyes. He looked like a man with many regrets.

She knew well the weight of that burden. "Please, don't worry about it."

"The girls will replace it." His tone brooked no argument, but it wasn't harsh. "About what my daughters said to you."

"Do you mean their proposal? Don't worry. It's plain to see they are simply children longing for a mother's love."

"Thank you for understanding. Not many folks do."

"Maybe it's because I know something about longing. Life never turns out the way you plan it."

"No. Life can hand you more sorrow than you can carry." Although he did not move a muscle, he appeared changed. Stronger, somehow. Greater. "I'm sorry the girls troubled you, Miss McKaslin."

Mrs., but again she didn't correct him. It was the sorrow she carried that stopped her from it. She preferred to stand in the present with sunlight on her face. "It was a pleasure, Dr. Frost. What blessings you have in those girls."

"That I know." He tipped his hat to her, perhaps a nod of respect, and left her alone with the restless wind and the door still open in her heart.

* * * * *

Love Inspired SUSPENSE

RIVETING INSPIRATIONAL ROMANCE

Agent Brice Whelan's mission is simple: save missionary/nurse Selena Carter. But Selena's run-in with a drug cartel puts her in danger—danger that doesn't end once she's back home. Brice needs to keep her safe and that means staying by her side...whether she wants him there or not.

Look for

CODE *of* HONOR

by **LENORA WORTH**

Available April wherever books are sold.

Steeple Hill®

LIS44333

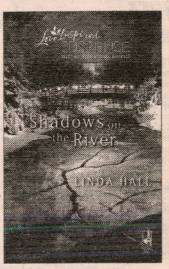

REQUEST YOUR FREE BOOKS!

2 FREE INSPIRATIONAL NOVELS
PLUS 2
FREE
MYSTERY GIFTS

Love Inspired.

YES! Please send me 2 FREE Love Inspired® novels and my 2 FREE mystery gifts (gifts are worth about $10). After receiving them, if I don't wish to receive any more books, I can return the shipping statement marked "cancel". If I don't cancel, I will receive 4 brand-new novels every month and be billed just $4.24 per book in the U.S. or $4.74 per book in Canada, plus 25¢ shipping and handling per book and applicable taxes, if any*. That's a savings of over 20% off the cover price! I understand that accepting the 2 free books and gifts places me under no obligation to buy anything. I can always return a shipment and cancel at any time. Even if I never buy another book, the two free books and gifts are mine to keep forever.

113 IDN ERXA   313 IDN ERWX

Name	(PLEASE PRINT)	
Address		Apt. #
City	State/Prov.	Zip/Postal Code

Signature (if under 18, a parent or guardian must sign)

Order online at www.LoveInspiredBooks.com

Or mail to Steeple Hill Reader Service:

IN U.S.A.: P.O. Box 1867, Buffalo, NY 14240-1867
IN CANADA: P.O. Box 609, Fort Erie, Ontario L2A 5X3

Not valid to current subscribers of Love Inspired books.

Want to try two free books from another series?
Call 1-800-873-8635 or visit www.morefreebooks.com

* Terms and prices subject to change without notice. N.Y. residents add applicable sales tax. Canadian residents will be charged applicable provincial taxes and GST. Offer not valid in Quebec. This offer is limited to one order per household. All orders subject to approval. Credit or debit balances in a customer's account(s) may be offset by any other outstanding balance owed by or to the customer. Please allow 4 to 6 weeks for delivery. Offer available while quantities last.

Your Privacy: Steeple Hill Books is committed to protecting your privacy. Our Privacy Policy is available online at www.SteepleHill.com or upon request from the Reader Service. From time to time we make our lists of customers available to reputable third parties who may have a product or service of interest to you. If you would prefer we not share your name and address, please check here.

LIREG08R

Love Inspired

TITLES AVAILABLE NEXT MONTH

Available March 31, 2009

TWICE UPON A TIME by Lois Richer
Weddings by Woodwards

Between his work and his twin boys, widower Reese Woodward has no time for love. Or so he thinks until he meets Olivia Hastings, his sister's best friend. Her past makes her wary of romance, but who can resist the adorable twins—or their father? Together they might find their second chance for a doubly blessed happy-ever-after.

TEXAS RANGER DAD by Debra Clopton
A Mule Hollow Novel

When Texas Ranger Zane Cantrell returns to Mule Hollow after years away, he comes face-to-face with the son of an old girlfriend—who also happens to be his son! Zane can't believe Rose Vincent kept this secret from him all these years. But he's eager to get to know his boy, and to prove he's never stopped loving Rose. Can they build a brand-new life together?

HOMECOMING BLESSINGS by Merrillee Whren

Small-town girl Amelia Hiatt and big-city businessman Peter Dalton think they have nothing in common. When they team up on a special project, they soon realize they're more alike than they could ever imagine. Except the big-city bachelor isn't ready to settle down, and Amelia is ready for a family of her own. But she's determined to change his mind—and his heart.

READY-MADE FAMILY by Cheryl Wyatt
Wings of Refuge

Ben Dillinger is used to playing the hero to damsels in distress, he's just not used to falling in love with them! When the pararescue jumper rescues single mom Amelia North and her daughter from a car accident, Ben realizes he's found the family he's been longing for. And he'll do whatever it takes to prove to her that he's the missing piece in her ready-made family.

LICNMBPA0309